"The lives of three women in pain—a doctor in New York, a young widow in Austin, and a serial killer on a Texas death row—are the unlikely subjects of this compelling literary Austinite debut. Ward follows these three characters as their social orbits incredibly but inexorably draw closer day by day. Ward weaves her complex plot into a seamless whole. And, despite the deeply emotional subject matter, the story never bogs down in sentimentality. Death row has never looked so real. Victims' rights have never felt so tragically violated."
—MIKE SHEA, *Texas Monthly*

"The compelling *Sleep Toward Heaven* features razor-sharp writing and characters that are believably rendered. Faith, forgiveness, and redemption comprise tried-and-true terrain in fiction. Ward delivers all three without manipulation or melodrama. She has woven a wonderful fictional tapestry with meaning embedded in the threads."
—*Fort Lauderdale Sun-Sentinel*

"Amanda Eyre Ward tackles her subject with sensitivity . . . opening doors into a world unobserved by most. But it is Ward's compassion that makes this small novel such a powerful experience, for she embraces them all, frailties and flaws, with a singular clarity."
—CurledUp.com

"Ward captures the essence of three very distinct women whose lives are inextricably bound together. With a voice that is crystal clear and resounds long after you've finished the book, *Sleep Toward Heaven* is a marvel."
—BookPeople bookstore (Austin, TX)

"This is a book that grabbed me from the get-go."
—*Poisoned Pen*

D0028706

"Ward works with a film editor's pace, snipping and cutting quickly between the three women as they each try to piece together lives which have been shattered by violence and disappointment. The result is a novel that reads like lightning, but has the lasting roll of thunder."

—CultureDose.com

"My fellow reviewers are calling this book extraordinary, and they are right. There are some incredibly placed words in this book; every chapter, every paragraph is crafted with perfect care. . . . Ward does not throw down the soapbox and preach against or even for the death penalty, which would cheapen the experience—she tells each story with honesty and beauty, allowing us to decide within ourselves what is right. . . . I am still reeling over the experience of this book. It is a work of elegant prose."

—MostlyFiction.com

Praise for
Sleep Toward Heaven

"Ward's no-nonsense, unflinching prose and her complex but never confounding structure make this novel very tough to put down. But her greater triumph is her ability to humanize all these characters. In their hope and their humor . . . we cannot help but see ourselves."

—PAM HOUSTON, *O, The Oprah Magazine*

"It's funny and sad and redemptive. Read it now. Thank me later."

—JENNIFER WEINER, *New York Times*
bestselling author of *Good in Bed*

"Hauntingly rich, wise and sharply etched."

—JAMES ELLROY

"*Sleep Toward Heaven* is a merciful gaze on the lives of three women inextricably linked by murder and ultimate grace. Brutal, beautiful, wise—Amanda Eyre Ward has written a storm of a novel. It will rattle the cage of your heart."

—DEBRA MAGPIE EARLING, author of *Perma Red*

"In this ambitious debut novel, with cinematic scope and a probing eye, Amanda Eyre Ward takes her readers inside the criminal justice system and into the hearts and minds of three women whose lives literally hang in each other's hands during a few desperately hot months of Texas summer."

—THISBE NISSEN, author of *Out of the Girls' Room and into the Night* and *The Good People of New York*

"This is a terrific read, involving and surprising. Ward gives us a textured, vivid portrait of women on death row. Her writing is unflinching, sometimes hauntingly funny, always compelling."

—KAREN STOLZ, author of *Fanny and Sue* and *World of Pies*

"Sometimes the best fiction is inspired by fact, as in the case of *Sleep Toward Heaven*, a first novel that manages to be both socially relevant and completely personal . . . wonderfully sewed to the fringe of autobiography, in this case searching for an answer to the question: 'Is that darkness within me?'"

—*New York Post*
(named one of five new writers to watch)

"How do we forgive the unforgivable? First-time novelist Ward explores this question with a delicate blend of compassion, humor, and realism. Ward's celebration of human resilience never becomes preachy, sentimental, or politically heavy-handed. Her spare but psychologically rich portraits are utterly convincing."

—*Publishers Weekly*

"Ward's impressive debut novel is a powerhouse of melancholic emotions channeled through the jagged lives of her intricate cast of female characters. Ward deftly creates a route by which all three women irrevocably touch each other's lives, their sorrow reaching through the darkness like searching fingers on the hand of destiny."

—*Booklist*

"In *Sleep Toward Heaven*, gifted writer Amanda Eyre Ward intertwines the lives of three women in a poignant tale of benevolence and brutality, whose compelling images resonate long after the final page has been turned. Her sharply drawn characters ponder life's capital-letter concepts—Guilt, Vengeance, Forgiveness. Her tone is masterfully restrained, impassioned without being preachy, and darkly humorous. Surging swiftly toward the inevitable, Ward's astonishing debut blends pathos and suspense into the rarest of fictional breeds—a literary page-turner."

—*BookPage*

© Dennis Hearne

About the Author

AMANDA EYRE WARD was born in New York City and graduated from Williams College and the University of Montana. Her short stories have been published in various literary reviews and magazines, including the *Austin Chronicle, Tin House* magazine, *StoryQuarterly,* Salon.com, the *Mississippi Review,* and the *New Delta Review.* Ward is a contributor to the *Austin Chronicle.* Visit her at www.amandaward.com.

sleep toward heaven

a novel by
Amanda Eyre Ward

📚 Perennial

An Imprint of HarperCollins*Publishers*

"Sleeping Toward Heaven" © 1987 William Stafford from *An Oregon Message* (Harper & Row). Reprinted by permission of The Estate of William Stafford.

A hardcover edition of this book was published in 2003 by MacAdam/Cage Publishing. It is here reprinted by arrangement with MacAdam/Cage Publishing.

HarperCollins books may be purchased for educational, business, or sales promotional use. For information please write: Special Markets Department, HarperCollins Publishers Inc., 10 East 53rd Street, New York, NY 10022.

First Perennial edition published 2004.

Designed by Dorothy Carico Smith

Library of Congress Cataloging-in-Publication Data
Ward, Amanda Eyre.
    Sleep toward heaven : a novel / Amanda Eyre Ward.—1st Perennial ed.
    p. cm.
    ISBN 0-06-058229-4
    1. Executions and executioners—Fiction. 2. Murder victims' families—Fiction. 3. Death row inmates—Fiction. 4. Women librarians—Fiction. 5. Women physicians—Fiction. 6. Women murderers—Fiction. 7. Widows—Fiction. 8. Texas—Fiction. I. Title.

PS3623.A725S58 2003b
813'.6—dc22
                                                          2003060899

04 05 06 07 08 ❖/RRD 10 9 8 7 6 5 4

For Tip, my love.

While they slept, faith flowered, an outside dream,
and surrounded them in their cave. All they had to do
was to sleep toward Heaven and open their eyes
like dolls. Up there on the ceiling was all they needed.

—*William Stafford*

part one
june

karen

On Wednesday, they begin to get ready for the Satan Killer, who is due to arrive after lunch. They order a lamp and a radio from the commissary, and charge them to Tiffany's account. Karen makes the bed in the empty cell with clean sheets. All the women on Death Row, who had been using the cell as a storage room, have removed their belongings to give the Satan Killer a fresh start.

Lifting the sheet in the air and snapping it tight over the mattress, Karen remembers the pure relief that flooded through her when she first saw her own cell: bare, clean, and smelling of ammonia. It was almost five years ago.

Tiffany takes two books from the bookshelf, *Women Who Kill* and *The Jane Fonda Workout*. She puts them by the Satan Killer's bed. "There," she says.

It is four-thirty in the morning. Breakfast is over, and there is the long, pre-lunch stretch ahead of them. Tiffany stands outside the vacant cell, one thin arm around her stomach and the other against her chin. "Should I, like, draw her a picture or something? It looks so sad."

"Leave it alone," says Karen.

"But it looks pathetic," says Tiffany. She shakes her Farrah Fawcett hairdo, and it settles back into place. Underneath her white jumpsuit, her limbs are strong. Tiffany runs in place and does sit-ups and push-ups inside her cell. She takes recess daily, has made a dusty path the shape of the number eight in the small, fenced yard. She believes that she will be set free, and the belief makes her restless. Karen recognizes the sharp hope, like a piece of gravel in a shoe. The knowledge of time, and of missing out. When you let go of the hope, there is a dull, numb peace in its wake.

"Leave it alone," says Karen.

They live in a row, in Mountain View Unit. They share the television and the table bolted to the rectangle of cement in front of their cells. During the day, they are locked into the cage, where they work. Unlike the rest of the prisoners, they are not taught skills for the future. Instead, they make dolls called Parole Pals, which prison employees can special-order, choosing hair color, skin color, an outfit. All afternoon in the cage, the women paint faces on the Parole Pals, and make tiny clothes and shoes. Sometimes, Karen wakes in the night and sees the naked, faceless dolls that hang above the sewing machines. She has to remind herself that they are not babies, and not alive.

◆ ◆ ◆

Veronica agrees with Tiffany. She says, in her low, hoarse voice, "That cell certainly does need something. Something decorative." Veronica has been on Death Row the longest, and has a manner that commands respect, something about the way she holds her shoulders back and peppers her statements with words like "certainly," "absolutely," and "indeed." She is sixty-three years old, and wears her white hair in a bun. Her skin is loose, and she is fleshy, wide at the hips.

She rises from her cot and wraps one of her veined hands around a metal bar. Although they are no longer allowed cigarettes, Veronica has retained a smoker's way of speaking, pausing between statements, a pause that should be punctuated by a deep inhale and elegant exhale of smoke. They wait, and Veronica decrees, "Art."

"Excuse me?" says Karen.

"Art," says Veronica. "Everyone find something or make something. Some sort of art."

"Let her do it herself," says Karen. She points to Veronica's cell. "You don't want someone else's crap on your wall, you know?"

Veronica turns to look at her cell, which is filled with yellowing photographs. She has wedding pictures of herself with all her husbands: Allen, Grady, Bill, Patrick, Stephen, another Bill, Chuck. In the earliest pictures, she is small-boned, engulfed in dresses like cakes, layered and creamy. Over the years, her body grows solid and her wedding dresses become darker and more spare. Patrick is the last husband for whom she wore a veil. Veronica's face goes slack looking at the photographs. She is lost in one of her wedding days, spinning on a dance floor while the band plays "Starlight Melody" and her new husband presses his warm lips to her forehead.

Tiffany jumps in. "I wish you had put something in my cell. It was so horrible, being dragged here and dumped like a bag of garbage!" Her voice goes shrill, indignant. Tiffany insists that she is innocent, that somebody else drowned her daughters, Joanna and Josie. Somebody else took them to the pond behind Tiffany's house and put rocks in the girls' matching sleeping suits. Somebody threw them in, held them under until they drowned, and watched them sink. Their open mouths, throats filled with water. Eyes open to stinging darkness. In Tiffany's cell, she has twenty-six shades of nail polish, lined up in a gleaming row.

Karen tries not to roll her eyes. Jackie looks up from her sewing. "What about one of my quilts?" she says. "It would add some color, anyway." She brushes her hair from her freckled forehead with a quick motion, and something in her jaw snaps. Jackie is filled with mean energy. She moves fast, talks fast, has bony elbows and knees. To keep her hands moving, she sews: quilts, pillows, the dress she will be executed in. The dress is red, with sequins she orders from a catalog.

They will only let her have one dull needle, so her sewing goes pretty slowly. Although "Mountain View Quilts" seemed like a good idea for a business, Jackie has only sold one through the Web site her sister maintains. Jackie used to be a hairdresser, and likes to do everyone's hair.

Obviously, she can't cut anything, but she brushes it around and sprays hairspray. Also, she does Tiffany's nails. She is due to be executed in a month.

"I think the Satan Killer would love a quilt," says Tiffany, looking at Veronica.

"She can have this green one," says Jackie. "It's all fucked up." She gestures to a quilt that is uneven and badly stitched.

Karen reaches both arms behind her and pulls her thin ponytail taut. "Fine," she says. "Go ahead and make some art."

Veronica is still staring at her photographs. She does this: fades from the situation at hand. They all assume Veronica won't make anything for the empty cell. Besides disguising the taste of arsenic in home-cooked dinners, she isn't really talented in domestic arts.

They have already seen the Satan Killer on TV. She is black, like Karen. Her name is Sharleen Jones. She is nineteen years old.

Karen, who since childhood has been unable to ignore the dark edges around every situation, had a terrible dream about the Satan Killer. It was after her shower, the tooth powder still gritty in her mouth. Karen lay down on her cot, and the dream came to her unbidden: the thick forest where the children crouched, frightened, around a campfire. The air was hot and wet, and smelled like things growing.

In the dream, Sharleen looked kind. She wore jeans and a sweatshirt with a teddy bear on it. Sharleen's hair was parted in the middle and stuck behind her ears. She was dark-skinned, with brown eyes. Her shoulders were wide, like a man's. At her throat, a necklace rested, her name spelled in gold.

Karen saw it all in the dream: Sharleen, her boyfriend, and the four small children walking down the trail and then into the undergrowth. Pine needles against their cheeks, the lifeless limbs of a dead tree. It was hard to make a fire. Sharleen took the clothes off the children, peeled them off, like fruit. Folded them (small pants, shirts, socks, boots, hats) and put them in a paper bag. The pattern of leaves against the darkening sky, flickers of light from the smoldering fire. Sharleen's voice, high, chanting, a glinting knife, and the blood. Karen woke from the dream to the screaming from the mental ward down the hall.

One day the guards forgot to change the channel, and the women on Death Row watched Sharleen's trial with rapt attention. Karen already knew, but found that she had been right: each child had been sliced across the throat, their hearts cut from their bodies.

Jackie unfurls the ugly quilt and smoothes it over the Satan Killer's bed. Veronica has decided to pencil something onto paper in a fancy script. So far, she has written "S" and "E." *Sex?* wonders Karen, *Seagull? Secret?*

Tiffany fancies herself a painter, and has settled at the picnic table with her watercolor set. She appears to be painting a bird of sorts, with long talons. When she dips her brush in the bowl of water, color streams from it like smoke.

"You're not going to do anything?" Jackie is standing in

front of Karen's cell, her eyes narrowed scornfully. Karen rolls over on her cot to face the wall. "Bitch," says Jackie.

The Satan Killer arrives at two. Tiffany and Veronica are at showers, and Jackie is sewing her sequins. Between the guards' strong arms, Sharleen looks like a giant rag doll. She lets her head loll forward, exposing the bare skin where her hair parts, and is dragged to her cell, putting up no resistance. The guards are Keith and Edward, both new.

Guards do not stay for long on Death Row. When they find themselves smiling at a joke from Tiffany, or giving Karen extra cups of tea, the guards seem to know that it is time. Something happens to them. Their skin grows soft; the sadness seeps inside them. They are replaced. The guards that remain are solid as steel.

Sharleen sinks down onto her cot, and Karen thinks she can hear crying. Jackie is always mean, as mean as a snake. She puts down her sewing, runs her hands through her red mane, and saunters over. Karen closes her eyes.

"You the Satan Killer?" Jackie asks. She gets no answer from Sharleen. "I made you that quilt," says Jackie. Again, there is no reply. "I made you that fucking quilt!" says Jackie. She has to shout to be heard above the television. Jackie walks to the middle of the room and stretches. Her white prison clothes are loose. She begins to practice high kicks. "I could have been a dancer," she says. "Everybody said so." She kicks and kicks until she is out of breath, and then she goes back to Sharleen.

Don't blame Jackie. She is so tired of sequins. She has

sewn three hundred and seventeen sequins. She has been on Death Row for ten years, has made twelve quilts, and is going to die. There has been no stay of execution, and the news says there will not be one. The TV shows a picture of Jackie with her hair like fire and then they show the governor with his tight mouth and smiling eyes. The governor says, "Tough on crime" and "Eye for an eye." No, there will be no stay for Jackie. They have not executed a woman in Texas since 1863, when they hung a woman named Chipita Rodriguez for murdering a horse trader.

"Satan Killer?" says Jackie. "Why don't you answer me?"

It seems to Karen that Sharleen is asleep. She faces the wall in her cell, and has her knees drawn up. Karen tries to remember being nineteen. She had not yet met Ellen, and had just started to turn tricks, still got high from beer. Karen remembers being on a bus, eating a cheeseburger half-wrapped in paper. She had been going from Houston to New Orleans, and had hope inside her. It makes Karen's head hurt to think of those times, before she had known that life would always suck, no matter where you went or who was sticking it in you.

Jackie is getting worked up. She kicks at the bars of Sharleen's cell. "Wake the fuck up, Satan Killer!" she says, over and over again. When Sharleen does not move, Jackie goes inside the cell.

Between breakfast and bedtime, their cell doors are open so they can stretch and walk around the three hundred square feet of concrete, which they call "the patio." Their cells line one side of the patio, and a metal table and chairs are attached to the concrete. Above the table is the television, bolted high on the wall. Opposite the cells is the chute, where the guards watch the women's movements and listen to their words. Next to the cells the cage, which is kept locked whether or not the women are inside it, holds the row of sewing machines.

Jackie sits on the floor next to Sharleen's bed. "Why don't you answer me?" she says, right in Sharleen's ear.

There is a muffled reply.

"Because you what?" says Jackie.

Sharleen whispers again, a faint sound that Karen cannot make out.

"Damn *right* you scared!" says Jackie. She laughs, and then her laughter stops. All Karen can hear is a smack, and then another sound, more like a thud against concrete. Then there is only the sound of the TV laughing.

The guards from the chute come running, and then there are more guards, and then a stretcher. Sharleen's voice is quiet and small and she tells them that Jackie fell and hit her head on the floor. "I don't want no trouble," says Sharleen.

That night, they are all searched. While they stand in their underwear, they look at the floor, and do not talk to each other. Karen's underwear is worn and yellow, like Veronica's. Tiffany has Calvin Klein underwear, from her husband. Sharleen, who has a T-shirt instead of a bra, is big and muscular, just as she was in Karen's dream. She looks as if she could lift a house. Her legs shake when the guard sticks a finger in. When she has been searched, she goes right back to bed, turning her face to the wall. Above her bed is Tiffany's bird, wings spread in flight. Next to the picture is Veronica's word: SERENITY.

Karen thinks about things to say to Sharleen. She wants to tell her that she is not alone in knowing what it feels like to tear through human life. She wants to tell Sharleen that hatred ebbs to a steady ache. Instead, she mixes Tang with cream cheese from the commissary. The mixture is bright and soft. She spreads it on a plate, takes only a mouthful, and slides the plate into Sharleen's cell.

Sharleen, she does not say, there is such joy in breathing out, knowing you can breathe in again.

franny

The graveyard smelled of fresh earth and rain. Franny's face was raw, her hair wet knives on her cheek. She balled her hands inside her coat pockets and willed herself not to cry. The priest said something about God's plan, and mystery. There was no mystery about it. Franny bit the words down. It was cancer, it had metastasized, eaten Anna's cells, refused every form of therapy, even burning the marrow from her bones. "God's mystery," whispered Franny, closing her eyes. If only she could believe in such a thing.

Anna's father was sobbing, his mouth open and his tongue exposed. Anna's mother stared straight ahead at the tiny coffin. She wore a black suit and her platinum hair seemed inappropriate, bright. Franny fought the urge to walk over to them, put Mr. Gillison's tongue back in his mouth and cover Mrs. Gillison's hair with something. That black piece of fabric on the coffin, maybe.

Franny had known they made coffins for children, of course she had known, but the shock of seeing one put to use had almost made her cry out. The coffin was shiny, covered in flowers and Beanie Baby dolls. Franny had not attended the open-casket wake. According to Clyde, they had put a wig on Anna, the long red curls she had missed so dearly.

The priest stopped talking, and the funeral man stood by with a big frown on his face. He shook his head dramatically, as if he cared, as if he didn't go to ten funerals a day.

The graveyard was a vibrant green. The Gillisons' friends were well-dressed, weepy, and shell-shocked. Many of them had visited Anna in the hospital, and Franny recognized their faces: the woman in the cape had brought Anna a puzzle, the heavyset man had brought macadamia nut cookies. (Anna had eaten them all and then puked them up half an hour later, Franny's fingers stroking Anna's bare head.) Franny stood away from the crowd, alone. She knew how they felt, and she felt the same way: it was her fault.

Mrs. Gillison stepped forward to say something, took a breath, but then just stood and stared, twisting something in her hands: a Beanie Baby? It flashed, dull orange, through her fingers. Franny saw it was the lion, Anna's favorite. Finally, Anna's mother reached out with a trembling hand to place the doll on the coffin. She let go too early, recoiling from the hole in which her daughter would be buried, and the lion fell, missing the coffin, into the earth.

"Get it out," she said, and then she began to scream, "Get it out! Get it out!" The funeral man looked dismayed. Franny could see him weighing his options.

Finally, someone stepped forward. An uncle, Franny

thought. He knelt in the wet grass, and reached underneath the coffin, rooted around. Everyone was frozen. This was not supposed to happen at a funeral. It was too much.

Franny pressed her thumb down on her engagement ring. The diamond cut into her finger, and she pushed until she felt her skin tear. The muddy lion was back in Mrs. Gillison's hands, and Mr. Gillison was trying to take it away. Everyone looked on nervously, they really had to be going, there was a football game tonight, and dinner to be prepared and eaten, sex with your lover, life, life. Franny wanted a drink. A cigarette.

Mrs. Gillison was holding tight to the lion. Mr. Gillison had stopped crying, and watched dumbly as the funeral man and his assistant began to turn the crank that would lower Anna's body into the ground. Ashes to ashes, dust to dust, the priest had said.

Franny had told Nat not to come to the funeral when he had offered. *You're too busy*, she told him. *Children may come and children may go, but the gigs go on.* She had smiled, as if this was a joke, and he had stared at her. She knew she wasn't being reasonable, but she didn't care. It was startling not to care, for she was a person who had always cared too much.

Oh, that little girl's body. Franny knew it, inside and out. The liver riddled with tumors, the stomach sour and mean, the eyes. Franny would never forget Anna's eyes: green with orange fire. They would lock with Franny's when the worst was on. And when Franny had nothing left to give, Anna's eyes had closed.

Clyde Duncan, Anna's official doctor, had given up on

Anna months before. He had walked in one afternoon when Franny was standing at Anna's bedside, watching Anna sleep. "Dr. Wren," Clyde had said. He put his hand on Franny's shoulder. "It's over," he said. And because of this—because Clyde had given up on Anna—Franny held on. But he had been right.

The rain pelted the small tent over the gravesite. Someone was making an announcement about refreshments. Refreshments! The Gillisons lived on the Upper East Side, Franny knew. She had been to their apartment when it still smelled of potpourri, and not of vomit. She had convinced Anna's parents to try the transplant. It was a faint hope, but a hope nonetheless. She remembered their pinched faces, their lost expressions, hands that wandered in their laps. "Just tell us what to do," Mr. Gillison had said.

When everyone was gone, Franny came closer to the grave. The funeral man and his assistant had dropped their sad looks and were discussing logistics, but as soon as she approached, their eyes filled with misery again. "Are you a relative?" said the assistant sadly, "a cousin, maybe?"

"No," said Franny, "I was her doctor." The funeral man stood up straight, and pushed his shoulders back.

"She was very sick," he said, finally. "I hear," he added.

"I made her go through a bone marrow transplant when there was no chance of her making it," Franny said. The man nodded, furrowed his brow, looked out the corner of his eye at his watch. "She could have died in peace," said Franny, "at home, with her family. But I wouldn't let her."

"The Lord works in mysterious ways," said the assistant.

"I burned the marrow out of her bones. She died in terrible pain. It was my fault." Franny looked up, and both men were staring at her. "I bet you hear a lot of graveside confessions," said Franny.

"Not really," said the funeral man, at the same time the assistant said, "Yes."

"Thank you," said Franny. She took a last glance at Anna's grave, and turned to go.

"Don't mention it," called the assistant.

The Gillisons' building had an elevator man. He was old, and had white hair. He smelled of cigars. "Seven," said Franny. He nodded and closed the elevator doors.

"Going to the Gillisons'?" he said.

"Yes."

The elevator man was silent until they'd reached the seventh floor. "That little tyke drove me nuts," he said. Franny turned to him and smiled. "She used to roller-skate in the lobby," he said.

"I have to go," said Franny.

The man opened the door. "Sure, sure," he said. "I always told her she'd kill herself, roller-skating in the lobby."

The door to the Gillisons' apartment was closed. Franny rang the bell, and a tall woman in a purple pantsuit opened the door. Her hair was braided and affixed to her head. "Come in, come in," she said, "I'm Carol's sister, Anna's aunt. And you are—"

"Franny Wren."

"Hello, hello," she said, and stretched her arm to point

to the bedroom. "You can put your coat…" She stopped. "Dr. Wren?" she said. Franny nodded. The woman pursed her lips, and crossed her arms. "I'd like to have a word with you," she said.

"Of course," said Franny.

"Would you like some wine?"

"Yes."

A young cousin was called to take Franny's coat, and Anna's aunt took Franny by the arm. In the dining room, platters of cheese and meat were laid out in circles, like eyes. There were rolls in a basket and bottles of wine lined up on the sideboard. Anna's aunt pulled a cork from a bottle of red wine with great effort and poured two glasses. She led the way through the crowd into the kitchen, where they could be alone. The kitchen was cluttered with Tupperware containers. A cat circled warily. Franny sipped her wine.

"My name is Georgina," said Anna's aunt. Franny nodded and smiled weakly. Georgina wore heels with pants, a look that Franny had always admired and been frightened of. "I'm a naturopath in Australia," said Georgina. *Here we go*, thought Franny. She took another sip of wine. The cat had begun to lick at a dish of what looked to be cream cheese. "I have some questions," said Georgina, her eyes flashing, "about my niece's course of treatment."

"The cat is licking the cream cheese," said Franny.

"What?" Georgina was almost shrieking.

"The cat," Franny repeated. She shook her head. "Forget it. Please, feel free to ask whatever you'd like."

"My primary concern," said Georgina, "is why a

naturopath was never consulted in the matter of Anna's ailment."

"That is a very interesting question," said Franny. She did not say, *And where were you?*

"Hm," said Georgina. It was the sound of a sniff.

"First of all," said Franny, taking a cookie from an open box on the counter, "I'm just finishing my residency. I took a special interest in Anna, but her primary doctor is actually Clyde Duncan." She took a bite of the cookie, a butter cookie lined with chocolate.

"You advised my sister, did you not?"

"Yes, I did. As I said, I took a special interest in Anna. I loved her, actually." Franny took another cookie. "I gave the best advice I could. I'm not well-trained in natural therapy, but of course the Gillisons were free to consult with whomever they wanted."

Georgina raised an eyebrow. "I think many alternative therapies can be very effective," said Franny, "but Anna's cancer was quite advanced." She felt tears, a hot ball in her throat. "There was really nothing that could be done." Franny chewed her cookie slowly. She felt it would be rude to crunch. Georgina nodded, thinking. The cat continued to lick the dish. On the refrigerator, a scrap of legal paper held up with a ladybug magnet: "TUESDAY, 4PM, A. TO DR. WREN."

Mrs. Gillison smelled of gin and Chanel No. 5. She held Franny too tightly for too long, and appeared to be shivering. "I know you did all you could," she said, "I know you did all you could." When she released Franny, she said,

"Would you like a shrimp roll?" Franny shook her head. They stood in the doorway between the living room and the dining room. People hovered nearby, pressing, keeping an eye on Mrs. Gillison. "You're the only one," said Mrs. Gillison, the ice in her glass clinking as she rocked it back and forth. "You're the only one who knows a thing."

Franny looked down. Mrs. Gillison drained her drink. A man took the glass for a refill. Keeping Mrs. Gillison good and drunk seemed to be the point. "She should have died here, though," said Mrs. Gillison. "We should not have let you take her back."

The man returned with a full glass of gin. "We should not," said Mrs. Gillison, "have given her *back*!" She stumbled, unbalanced by the volume of her voice, perhaps, but then righted herself, and patted her hair. "Thank you, Jimmy," she said to the man. After a deep sip, she asked, "Who's next?" and a mousy woman fell into her embrace.

Why didn't Franny go home? She had a fiancé, after all, and a cat. She had made her appearance and paid her respects. Why did she keep eating cookies and drinking wine? After a time, she found herself looking at the shiny forehead of a man who spoke to her intently. "And some people think I'm selfish," the man was saying.

"Excuse me?"

"It's not my fault that I can't be satisfied in a mono-gamous relationship," said the man. He shrugged, took his toothpick, and speared the olive in his glass. He chewed the olive with relish. "In some cultures," he said, "I'd fit right in, is the thing." He sighed, and Franny smelled a flat, sour smell. "You doing anything later?" said the man, "I mean, after this...this..."

"This wake?" said Franny.

"Well, yeah. Um, there's this great jazz club in Alphabet City."

Franny blinked. "I have got to leave now," she said.

Her coat was hanging in the bedroom. As she slipped it on, a voice came from a dark corner: "Do you know how many nights I sat here?"

It was Mr. Gillison. He was sitting on a windowsill, looking out at the building across the courtyard. "I sat here," he said, "and looked into all the other windows." He breathed in and out. He held a glass of dark liquid in his hand. "I thought of all the other lives, all the people, just on my block. And they have bad times, right? I mean, everyone has problems."

"Mr. Gillison," said Franny.

"Dr. Wren," said Mr. Gillison, and he turned and looked at her. His eyes were red and puffy. "I'm ashamed to say that I wished I could trade lives with any one of these people. Even that sad fuck." He pointed to a window that Franny could not see. She wanted desperately to leave, to be outside this apartment.

"That guy," said Mr. Gillison, "he's got nothing. He watches television and irons his shirts. He doesn't even have a plant. He's got nothing." Mr. Gillison laughed, but it was not a happy sound. It was a mean sound. "I'd give anything in this world," he said, "to trade my life with that man."

Franny sighed. "I'm so sorry," she said.

"I'm sorry, too," said Mr. Gillison.

"She should have died here, at home. It was my fault. I know that," said Franny.

"Yes," said Anna's father. "I know that, too."

The streets were slick and shining. Franny breathed in deeply, and decided to walk for a while. Though it was June, the air was cool. She bought a pack of cigarettes at a kiosk, and lit one in the shadows of an ATM machine. It was a bad idea to walk through the park at night, but she turned in anyway. The night was silent, but for Franny's footsteps and the wind in the trees.

On a bench, a figure was outlined in lamplight, completely still. Franny began to feel sick, and dropped her cigarette.

A man in a dress lurched by, murmuring. His dress was mauve taffeta. He wore no shoes, and his hair was long and matted. Franny walked faster, feeling heat rise underneath her arms. She broke into a run.

I don't think I want to live anymore, Anna had said, and then, *Don't tell my mom.* Franny shushed her, ran fingers over her scalp, as soft as a newborn's. *You do want to live,* she said, *yes, sweetheart, you do.* Anna had not answered.

Her little feet. Her slippers were blue, and lined in lamb's wool. Anna liked hot chocolate, pizza, and Gobstoppers. She did not like mushrooms. They were slimy, but she liked sushi, which was also slimy, so it didn't make sense. Wasabi sauce was too hot, but Anna liked the green sauce on tacos, the hottest sauce.

Anna's best friend was—had been—a girl named Kim. Kim had stopped visiting after the first chemo treatment, but she called, and Franny would hear Anna giggling on the phone. Kim had a boyfriend, Anna told Franny, so she was really busy. Kissing was slimy, like mushrooms, and Anna didn't think she would like it, but maybe she would change her mind.

Franny thought of her lab coat, its chemical smell, her stethoscope. She knew what had happened, knew exactly what Anna's body had done and had not been able to do. It was not God's mystery. It was not a mystery at all.

She stopped running and lit another cigarette. She was halfway across the park. Franny watched the smoke from her mouth circle toward a streetlight, disappearing. She walked steadily until she reached Central Park West.

In front of her building, a man in a dark coat waited. He nodded at Franny, and raised his arm for a taxi that did not stop. Franny pushed the door open and smelled meat cooking. She unlocked her mailbox: cable bill, laundry bill, postcard. Franny flipped the card. *Here I am in New Orleans! Remember Mardi Gras '90? See you in August, Big Boy.* The front of the postcard showed a Mardi Gras parade, a colorful float, a crowd of waving arms. One of Nat's friends. They lived in a world of parades, stretching one party to the next. Franny stood in her lobby, trying to believe that she could spend her life knowing them, laughing with them, planning vacations.

She wanted to be like the rest of the wives and girlfriends, giggling and rolling her eyes and pouring bags of corn chips into bowls.

The elevator was broken again. Franny climbed the stairs heavily. She unlocked the apartment door and flicked on the light. "Hello?" she called, "Nat?" There was no answer, but her cat, Ophelia, came running. "Hi, sweet," said Franny, scooping up Ophelia and holding the warm fur to her neck. Franny dropped the mail on the side table and walked into the kitchen. "Honey?" she called. On the kitchen table, there was a note written on the back of a bank statement: *Where are you? Got lonely—Went for a drink at Paddy's—Come join? N.*

Franny put down the note. She did not want to be filled with rage. Ophelia jumped from her arms and ran, leaving a scratch on Franny's hand, a line that filled with blood. "Fuck!" Franny cried. For a moment, she considered putting her coat back on, but the convivial scene unfolded before her—the dartboard, laughter ringing through smoke—and she shivered. No.

She opened the liquor cabinet and poured a hefty tumbler of Scotch. In the living room, she sank into the futon and turned on Nat's enormous television. A face filled the screen. "Oh, Lucy," said the face. "Do you really mean that?" Franny shut off the television. She gulped the whiskey, and put her head in her hands.

It came slowly, then, but steadily. The darkness. The anger Nat did not understand. It started in her gut, gathered force. She took another sip, tried to think of something else:

the wedding, a good steak, her Uncle Jack and his Old Spice smell.

It did not stop. It ran through her and over her, like a river. Anna was dead, she had died in the most horrible manner possible, and there was nothing, absolutely nothing, that Franny could do.

celia

Although my mother disagrees, I have moved forward with my life. For example, I've bought a new bikini. I do not know what possessed me to do it, but do it I did, late one night. I was watching TV (I had called the cable company and asked them to install every single channel possible. I figured I deserved the Movie Channel, HBO, Cinemax, and whateverall else. I deserved at least that). The show certainly did not lead to my decision; it was "Law & Order," and everyone was wearing chic coats as they fought injustice in cold climes. But summer was in the air in Texas, and I must have been thinking about the kids coming into the library for their summer reading books. Why the teachers insist on assigning books like *The Hobbit* I will never know. Those poor little ones with that thick tome. Nobody asks me for my opinion, but that's another story entirely. Summer, summer, summer.

I swiped the J.Crew catalog from the teachers' lounge when I dropped off some books at the elementary school on the other side of Austin. You'd think, being people who chose to spend their lives serving others at a menial salary, that the teachers would be nice. You'd be wrong. I have never met a group of such catty, unhappy people in my life. And they're not very bright. They spend all day leafing through catalogs, smoking, and saying how much they dislike their students and how they've got to lose weight. Every single one is on a diet. The juice diet, the rice diet, the cigarette and coffee diet. The only ones not on diets are pregnant. I've got to wonder, too: do they talk to their lovers the same way they talk to me, as if I were a dog that needed some training? "Oh, Celia, when you put coffee in the filter, *please* try not to spill it all over the counter. OK, honey?" It makes me want to smack them. And their Crayola-colored clothes!

My therapist, Maureen, says I have anger issues. She tells me that although I am through the official "Hostility" phase of my grieving process and full-on into the "Depression" and "Inability to Resume Business-as-Usual Activities" phase, I still "harbor intense reserves of uncontrollable anger." Maureen is a smart and insightful woman, and she may well be right, but I haven't smacked anyone, and that's a fact. I haven't taken heroin or tried to drown myself in a soapy tub. I ordered a bikini. Now, I ask you: doesn't that sound normal? It was on page thirty-four, a magenta stunner, worn by a WASPy girl with blonde hair tied into a ponytail. The girl was riding on the broad shoulders of a man who looked exactly like my high school boyfriend, George MacKenzie. Dark hair, chocolate eyes, that olive skin. God, I adored him. Last I heard he was a waiter at a Bennigan's outside Detroit, but the way he would make me come in the lunchroom when everyone else was in classes, rubbing right through my jeans! The few times I saw him asleep—once on a bus, during a school trip to a candlemaking factory, and once when we rented a hotel room after the prom—something opened in me, and a warmness slid in. Until he dumped me for some girl in Mississippi, where he went to college (before flunking out), I had a chance at being a warm human being. And I got a second chance. But now that's over.

So there I was, watching "Law & Order," drinking margaritas in my apartment on the south side of Austin. Outside, the sun had fully set, and the sound of cicadas rang like ripples around me. "Law & Order" was all about some cop who had murdered a lady in a restaurant, gone home, changed into his police uniform, returned to the restaurant, and then pretended to discover the body. Really, isn't life complicated enough?

So I looked down at the catalog, and there was the WASPy girl in the bikini, and it made me think of a better time. A time when I had never been dumped, for one thing, and when I had never been married and my husband hadn't been shot to death. A time when I didn't understand how fragile the whole world was, and how much could be taken away from you before you even realized what you had to lose.

The night my husband was murdered, I had wanted some beer. It was hot. This was long ago now, five years ago. But that night is clearer in my memory than last night, or the night before. The air smelled of grass. My husband had just cut the lawn. He was sticky and smelled like lawnmower fuel. He had blades of grass on his legs, glued to his socks and sneakers. He wore a big straw hat to keep the sun out of his eyes. Sitting on our porch swing reading a magazine— *Vanity Fair*—and petting our dog, Priscilla, I had watched him mow the lawn.

I'd won a bet—my husband had bet me that he could make Priscilla sit still with a biscuit on her nose, but he couldn't. Priscilla kept snapping her head around and eating the biscuit. I won the bet, so he had to go buy the beer. "Get something good," I yelled, as he pulled the truck out of the driveway. "None of that Miller Lite crap!" And that was the last word he heard from me: *crap*. I'm sure he heard some other words afterward, maybe a song on the radio, the price of the beer from the cashier. I can watch the tape if I want to find out exactly what Karen Lowens said. But the last word he heard from me, from his beloved wife, was "crap."

I called the J.Crew number and a cheery woman with a Southern accent answered the phone. She was very good-natured about the magenta bikini, which was not only available, but could be purchased with a small top and a medium bottom, what a deal! I gave her my credit card number and it was easy as that. I called my mother and told her the news and she seemed happy to hear it. "Just think," said my mother, in the middle of dinner with her new husband, a thousand miles away, "now you have something to look forward to!"

karen

Sharleen, they find out quickly, screams throughout the night. There's a long, earsplitting scream first, and then one or two whimpering cries. After a few nights, Karen finds a note in her cell after her shower. It is Veronica's handwriting: MEETING AT PATIO TABLE, TUESDAY DURING *LEEZA.* TO TALK ABOUT YELLING AT NIGHT.

They often write each other notes. There is something official, something polite and elegant, about the written word. Although they have all failed to live outside prison walls, they want to be considered polite. They write when there is something important to be said, something hard to say. Also, the guards cannot hear their letters. Though the guards will confiscate and read them later, the notes allow a fleeting sense of privacy.

On Tuesday, when Karen is waked by a guard with cold hands, the television is already on, a commercial for the ThighMaster. The guard smells like cigarettes and Vitalis.

Karen is handcuffed and led outside her cell. While the male guard goes through her books and drawings, a female guard's hands are searching her, inside, outside, cold hands. The other girls talk and scream, words and words, but Karen does not make a sound. They are searched six, sometimes eight times a day. Breakfast is a bun and cold coffee, maybe corn flakes with powdered milk. The coffee tastes like mud.

The Death Row inmates live next to the mentally ill prisoners, and can hear them, their voices like lost birds, rising and falling, the pepper spray, the mace.

After "Montel" ("Teen Sluts Speak Out"), they gather on the patio. There are only four chairs around the metal table. Jackie, busy sewing, is the last to arrive at the meeting, but instead of letting her sit on the floor, Karen stands up and gives Jackie her chair. They all know there will be enough chairs soon.

"I'm sorry to have to say this," says Veronica, her hands open on the table in front of the television, "but Sharleen, dear, this yelling has got to stop."

In her mind, Karen has assigned everyone a color. Karen herself is gray, no color. Veronica is black, because she is called the Black Widow on TV. Tiffany is pink, because everything is pink for her: bracelet, earrings, lips. Tiffany was tan before she came to Death Row, but now she is pale. She has bright blue eyes and hair the color of wheat. She looks like a Charlie's Angel, with her winged-out bangs and long legs.

"I keep waking up," says Tiffany breathlessly, "and hearing Sharleen screaming, and I think he's come back to get me!"

She puts her hand to her throat. Today her nails are Peach Zinger. "The man that killed my girls," she adds, for clarification.

"Yeah," says Jackie, "I keep thinking I'm hearing my husband from the grave." Jackie is red because her hair is red. It snakes out of any rubber band, frizzing upward, like vines. She says, "My fucking hair! It's alive, I'm telling you. I need conditioner. I just need some fucking conditioner."

Jackie hired a man to kill her husband and her two daughters. The man shot them and cut them up while Jackie was working at her beauty parlor, Get Snippy With Me. She says she was crazy then, but nobody believes her. She tells Veronica that she prays every night for another stay of execution.

"What the fuck do you want me to do?" says Sharleen. There is menace in her voice. For a nineteen-year-old, she is very scary. Karen decides that Sharleen will be purple.

"There's no need to swear," says Veronica.

Sharleen laughs. "You gotta be kidding me," she says.

"Sharleen," says Tiffany, "some of us are trying to live Christian lives here. Some of us are trying to be good people." Tiffany looks at Karen, the only one of them who does not attend Bible study. When the chaplain comes in the afternoons and everyone opens their Bibles around the patio, Karen goes into her cell.

Sharleen stands up from the table in a violent motion. "You think I wanna fucking scream?" she says in a strained voice. She looks at the chute, where the guards watch her steadily. She pinches her eyes closed and gathers her hands into fists. She is shaking. They all watch her, and wait. Even Veronica looks nervous. Sharleen takes a ragged breath, and then her hands unfurl and move down, tightly gripping the edges of the table. The table is bolted to the floor. Could she lift it, Karen wonders, and if she did, what would she do with it? Throw it across the room?

But Sharleen does not lift anything. Instead, keeping her hands wrapped around the edge, she opens her eyes. "You think you're safe in here, don't you?" she says in a low voice, too low for the guards to hear. "You think you're safe, all locked away from the world." She leans in, and her eyes narrow. "You think everyone who hates you is outside these walls," she says. "But you remember one thing. I'm in here with you."

Things were not always like this for Karen. Her earliest memory is her happiest one. She hopes that death will bring her back to that night, with the smell of her mother's breast: a powdery, caramel smell. The warmth of her mother's hair, ironed on the kitchen table. A car horn honking, a bright moon sky. Her mother whispering a lullaby, soft vowels, papery voice. They are in the rocking chair, on the porch, wooden boards squeaking. And Karen is inside her mother's arms. Is this a real memory? Is it any less real than the kicks to her stomach, the burns, the pricks shoving inside her? When she lies in her cell at night, when the TV is turned off and there is a lull in the noise, she thinks about the night on the porch. She tries to believe it was real. She counts the minutes until she will die. August twenty-fifth is sixty-two days away. 89,280 minutes.

franny

"**W**hy did you sleep on the couch?" Nat was awake first, as always, his hair unruly, his T-shirt smelling of sleep. Franny wanted to place her cheek next to his chest, to hear his heart, but something stopped her. Nat was slathering an English muffin with I Can't Believe It's Not Butter. He lifted his mug to his lips and drank. The metal percolator was plugged in. They had bought it at a tag sale in Connecticut from a woman in a wheelchair. "Answer the question," he said. He added, "Honey."

"Did you save me some coffee?"

He put down his mug. "Sorry."

"Do you even remember waking me up?"

"When?" He took a bite of the muffin.

"Forget it." Franny sat down at the kitchen table and ran a hand through her hair. Nat had come to her in the night, smelling of smoke and telling her he knew something was wrong. "What's wrong?" he had asked her in a slurred, sad voice. "What's wrong, Franny? What's wrong with us?" She felt guilty now about pretending to be asleep.

"How was the funeral?"

Franny sat up straighter. "It was difficult," she said. "But I'm OK."

"Are you really?"

"Yes." In silence, Franny made coffee. She emptied the grounds, refilled the pot, and plugged it in. She stood at the counter while it percolated, not looking at Nat. When it was ready, she poured a cup.

"Why don't you add sugar and cream, like you used to?"

"I don't know." She sank back down into her chair, one of a set they had been given as an engagement gift from Nat's parents.

"You did all right on the Scotch last night," said Nat, "and I found these in your purse." He held out the cigarettes.

"What were you doing in my purse?"

Nat paused. He sat down at the table, and leaned toward her. "I don't know."

"Don't go through my purse. Jesus!"

"I love you when you're angry," said Nat. Franny waited for the coffee to kick in. She sighed. Nat knelt next to Franny's chair and put his arms around her waist. He took Franny's chin in his fingers, turned her to him. "Franny, what's going on?"

"Nothing," said Franny. "I just want my coffee."

"Sweetie, look at you. Amelia is dead. It's okay for you to be down."

"Anna," said Franny, twisting her chin from Nat's grasp.

"What?"

"Her name is Anna," said Franny, her voice rising. "Anna!"

"Her name *was* Anna," said Nat.

"Fuck you," said Franny.

"Why won't you let me help you?" said Nat.

"Leave me alone," said Franny. "Can I just have my coffee, please?"

Nat snorted and shook his head. "You're a real piece of work," he said.

Franny liked to think things through. She made lists before she made decisions. After college, she had made a list of 157 careers she was suited for. She then spent twenty hours (drinking two pots of coffee before Uncle Jack cut her off) imagining each possible life. She winnowed the list to twenty-six (mourning each lost career: editor, dancer, real estate agent) when Uncle Jack told her she was going to medical school and sent her to bed.

In the morning, she had made a list of sixteen medical schools.

Now, on the subway, Franny took a pencil from her bag and tried to unravel the aching mess in her mind. She wrote, *Advil—need more.* She wrote, *funeral—bad idea.* She should not have gone to the funeral. She knew that what she had said to Mr. Gillison was inappropriate. He could go straight to the hospital and repeat her statement: "It was my fault." That polygamous man could testify to her many glasses of wine. Guilt sat heavily in Franny's stomach. She imagined her mentor, Jed Lewis, looking at her. "I am disappointed in you, Franny," he would say. And Uncle Jack, who had sacrificed everything to send her away from Gatestown. He had told her, after she had graduated from prep school and college, that it was up to her to make something of herself, to make something better of the world.

Franny gripped the pencil. *Not again. Stay professional, be strong,* she wrote. She resolved right then and there, the subway careening around a corner, picking up speed, that she would not let her emotions become tangled. Patients were bodies, cells, synapses, blood. She had to look at them as if they were jigsaw puzzles: *maybe if I put this piece at this angle...*She had always been good at jigsaw puzzles. It was the guessing games she had hated.

Jane Dikeman was brushing her hair in the hospital locker room. Franny smiled quickly, opened her locker, and pulled out her coat. "Franny?" said Jane, not turning from the mirror, gathering her hair into a ponytail, "I'm sorry. I'm sorry about that girl."

Franny shrugged and stared into her locker. She pressed her lips together. She looked at her apple shampoo, her red running shorts, dog-eared books. Her locker smelled like mold.

"Did you hear me?" said Jane.

Franny turned around. "It's fine," she said. In her own ears, her voice was breezy. "I'm fine," she said, pulling on her lab coat as she walked past Jane.

Franny's beeper sounded as she was gathering charts: Jed. She simply wasn't ready to talk to him. She needed more time. The charts swam in front of her eyes: diagrams, notes in her steady hand. Franny thought suddenly of Nat, of making love to him, covering him with kisses in a hot bathtub. Her knees went weak, and she grabbed the edge of the counter. She could hear her blood in her ears. She went quickly into the ladies' room, slipped into a stall. She pressed her face against the cool metal door.

Don't cry, she heard Uncle Jack tell her, his syllables long and slow. *Don't let them see you cry, Baby Doll.*

Jed was in his office, transcribing tapes. He was a tall man with skin the color of licorice. His coat had coffee stains on it, as usual, and something else: peanut butter? He was Franny's mentor, the chief internist, and one of her only friends. "Hello?" Franny tapped at the door.

"Franny, come in." He stood, snapped off his recorder, and took a pile of papers off a seat, gesturing for Franny to sit down. "I'm sorry about the Gillison girl."

Franny nodded. "I want you to know," she said, "that I'm fine. I'm fine."

Jed smiled, shook his head. "How could you be?" he said. He closed his door, blocking them from view.

"Well, I'm not going to…"

"What?" said Jed.

"I became involved, I guess, in a way that I won't again," said Franny.

Jed looked at her. "I know," he said.

"Dr. Duncan seemed so distant. As if he'd given up on Anna. I tried to step in, to…" Franny stopped and looked at the floor. "I know that I can't think of my patients as—"

"As human? Good luck, Fran. I remember the first patient I lost," said Jed. "Randall Eggers. He was a professional golfer. We talked about golf. I misdiagnosed his tumor as a headache. By the time my attending gave him a CT, he had lost months, maybe a year of his life." Jed took a sip of the coffee on his desk, made a face, and spit it back. "Don't want to know how old that is," he said.

"Thanks, Jed. I—"

"Franny, listen, you're going to care. We're not robots." He paused, as if searching for words that she could keep. "Don't take it home with you," he said, "That's one thing. I lost Rachel that way. Don't let that happen to you and Nat." He sighed. "You have to turn it off," he said. "It's like a faucet, Franny, and you let it run, and then you turn it off and go home."

"I can turn it off," said Franny, and she knew it was true.

"Good," said Jed. He seemed to be thinking of something else. "That's good for you," he said.

That weekend, Franny woke in Nat's parents' house, on Milton Road, in Rye, New York. It was six weeks before their wedding. She could smell Nat's family downstairs: the bacon sizzling, the lime aftershave splashed on his father's pitted cheeks, the salty smell of Porter, the Labrador, and Nat's mother's perfume—Safari. Coffee, Lemon Pledge, ocean. Downy fabric softener, blooming dogwood trees, butter. The smell of Westchester County, so different from the heavy, scorched smell of Texas. The June morning was warm, and the sea crashed outside the window, its breezes snapping the sails of the boats lined up along the swaying dock. Nat's family's house was right on the water, and if Franny were to open her eyes, she would see Long Island Sound. *I am so lucky to be here,* thought Franny, willing herself to believe it.

In her head, she made a list of the things she did feel: *trapped, nervous, apprehensive, sad.* She wanted to slip out of the expensive sheets, tiptoe down the stairs, past the kitchen, out the front door with its huge brass knocker in the shape of an anchor, down the pathway to the wooden gate. Once outside the gate, she would hitch a ride in someone's BMW to the station and buy a ticket back to the city. She would find a new, clean apartment, and…But the fantasy ended there, alone in an empty apartment.

Ever since Uncle Jack had sent her to boarding school when she was sixteen, Franny had felt out of place. She could remember the first fall at Kent School in Connecticut: sunset-colored leaves, smirking boys in their blazers, girls with long hair and bangs that feathered just right. Franny had Texas clothes: stonewashed jeans, skirts made out of bright cotton with matching tops. She wore eyeshadow and pantyhose, used hairspray. She didn't know what people meant by *The Vineyard* or *Stratton.* When Franny woke in her dorm room, her body filled with dreams of the Gatestown prison, there was no one who would understand, the way her childhood friends had.

Franny made herself lose her accent in a matter of weeks, but sometimes she slipped, saying *pin* for *pen* or *fixing to* or *y'all.* The other girls made fun of her curling iron and the sweater sets Uncle Jack had bought for her in Waco. One night, when the dorm had a "white trash party," two girls stopped by Franny's room, asking to borrow her clothes.

Franny learned. By her senior year, she was as snide as the rest, and wore Birkenstocks and Indian-print skirts. She Robo-ed, drinking a bottle of Robitussin cough medicine and hallucinating. She chewed tobacco, because the prefects couldn't smell it the way they could cigarette smoke.

At Yale, just three hours from Kent, Franny could talk about ski lodges, and about who was *so Choate* and who was *Miss Halls all the way.* She used words like *sweet* and *whatever.* When she went home on rare occasions, she felt out of place in Texas, superior to her old classmates and her beloved Uncle Jack. By the time she met Nat, she didn't belong anywhere. She wanted to escape Nat's house and their impending marriage: escape, the faint hope that the next place would be better, was her only comfort.

When do you stop trusting the instinct to run? Franny wondered. When do you accept that you will never feel at home, no matter where you go? When do you just make yourself stay?

"Franny?" Nat's voice was loud outside the guest room door.
"I'm awake."

The door opened, and Nat came inside. He held out a cup of steaming coffee to her. He had circles under his eyes, and his hair stood up in tufts. "Are you happy, Miss Bride?" he asked.

Franny sat up in bed. "How could I not be?" she said, holding out her hands for the cup.

"I never know what you mean when you say things like that," said Nat. His face darkened. He still wore his pajama pants and his Williams sweatshirt.

"Things like what?"

"I just wish," said Nat, crossing his arms over his chest, "that you could say, 'Yes, I'm happy.'"

The coffee was black and strong. In the mirror across from the bed, Franny could see herself. She looked thin, and she looked tired, but she did not look happy. "Nat, I am," she said.

"Oh," said Nat coldly. "Glad to hear it."

Franny heard the sound of a car pulling into the driveway. It was either the florist or the caterer.

"We're going to be so happy together," said Franny. She felt no corresponding flicker of joy. She smiled wide, so wide that her cheeks hurt.

"We are," said Nat forcefully. He came close to her and touched his lips to the top of her head. "I really do love you, sweetie," he said. "Can you just relax?"

"I am relaxed, Nat."

He stopped with his hand on the doorknob. "Franny?" His voice was nervous, and when his eyes caught hers, it seemed that he wanted to say something else, but he was silent.

"Nat," said Franny, "I am relaxed." And when he left her alone, closed the door behind him, for a moment, she was.

"Darling," said Nat's mother, Arlene, "I'm afraid I really don't see what the big problem is. Tulips are lovely flowers! In fact," she leaned in, as if sharing a secret, "I carried a bouquet of tulips at my own wedding to Frederick."

The florist, a squat woman named Reed, sighed. "Hon," she said, "I did everything I could. You changed the order too late."

"I wanted lilies from the beginning. Remember when I told you that my mother's name was Lily?" asked Franny, quietly. The kitchen was unbearably bright, and she wished she had a pair of sunglasses. There was a dull ache behind her eyes.

"No, dear, I don't. Anyway, won't the tents be lovely?" said Arlene. Her new facelift had given her a sinister look, her eyebrows always arched. She clasped her hands together. "Well!" she said.

Reed bit her lip and studied her nails. A rhinestone chip was embedded in each one. Outside, Franny saw Nat and his father arguing. Nat's hands were splayed, and he was shouting. His father was shaking his head. Franny couldn't hear anything above the sound of the waves.

"I'll handle this," Arlene was saying to the florist.

"I'm not trying to be difficult," said Franny.

"No, honey. Of course you're not!" cried Arlene. To Reed, she mouthed, "Nerves."

"It's going to be beautiful. It's going to be perfect. I promise, hon," said Reed with practiced cheer.

Arlene had made them hair appointments at Pierre's at eleven. "Pierre," said Arlene as she navigated her Land Rover to the salon, "is an absolute miracle worker." Franny decided to ignore the implications. Arlene waved as a friend drove by. "Oh, what an exciting day," she said, and then she turned to Franny. "Honey," she said, "let's have pedicures."

"I've never had a pedicure," said Franny.

"Welcome to Westchester, sweetie," said Arlene.

When Franny met Nat, during her second year of medical school, she was living near Columbia, in a tiny studio apartment she had painted green. One night, tired of studying alone in the medical library, Franny had wandered into a bar, promising herself that she would go home after one beer. But she had heard him, in the corner with the spotlight dimmed, his voice like molasses, singing quietly about darkness. She had ordered another beer, and then another. Franny thought, there is someone as sad as me, but he makes it beautiful.

Nat began to brighten her few free hours, winning Franny with homemade dinners, goofy songs, and tequila. He took her to parties where native New Yorkers talked quickly and sarcastically, and Franny, who had not been invited to any parties since losing touch with her few friends from college, was thrilled. While Nat spoke, his face animated, his fingers flying through the air like hummingbirds, she felt lucky, and could be still. Nat filled Franny's life with color; it bled into her exhausting days. She could stay up for the twelve-hour shifts, eating candy bars and vending machine sandwiches, sticking needles into veins, pretending to care about everyone's aches and pains. Knowing that her bright Nat waited for her, with an old movie or an invitation to a gallery opening, even tickets to the opera, she could handle anything. She loved to study, had a reason for it now: her life as a doctor would enable her to keep him happy. To keep him.

Franny rose to the top of her class. She chose internal medicine, and began to see patients more than just once, nice to meet you, jotting down notes, patient X. She began to take over cases, to know people's names, their smells, their nightgowns and bedside reading. Time slipped by, and she tried to ignore the sense that Nat's antics were becoming more desperate than joyous. His songs of sadness began to seem repetitive and indulgent to Franny. *Come to the hospital with me,* she wanted to tell him, when he played his most popular song, "Tears Like Snow," for the seven hundredth time. *I'll show you pain,* Franny thought.

Anna's death had changed something in Franny; everything seemed precarious. Franny vowed that Nat's sloppiness, his hangovers and his songs, would not stand in her way, or throw off the equilibrium of her carefully balanced life.

Pierre regarded Franny critically. He wore thick glasses and a long shirt with a belt around it. Franny's head had been massaged and shampooed, and a floral smell rose from her hair. "Nothing drastic," said Franny. "I'm getting married in August."

"The eyebrows, is what concerns me," said Pierre.

"Eyebrows?"

Pierre stood back, squinted, and then stood close again. He smelled of mint and cigars. "Tweezers!" he cried suddenly. A girl in a red smock rushed over. "You know," said Franny, "I really don't think…"

"Shhh," said Pierre. "Be calm." He breathed in slowly, lifting his palms, and then breathed out, dropping them. "You see? Yes?"

Franny nodded. The girl began to rub a hot lotion around her eyebrows, and Franny closed her eyes. Before long, the girl's fingers stopped, and Franny could smell Pierre again, feel his breath on her eyelids. She breathed in once, then out, and she felt a terrible pain as Pierre pulled eyebrow hairs from their sockets.

"Ouch!" Franny covered her eyes with her hands. She began, slowly, to cry.

"Oh dear," said Pierre, a hint of distaste in his voice. "My, my."

"I'm sorry," said Franny, "it's not the eyebrow."

"This girl," Franny heard Pierre whisper to Arlene, "she needs a nap, I think."

Arlene drove back to the house with bits of foil in her hair and her lips pressed together. At the gates to the house, she stopped. "Take a nap, now, will you?" she said. Franny nodded, and climbed out of the car. Arlene reversed so fast that Franny's shoes—Pappagallo sandals, which she had bought to fit in with the Westchester crowd—were covered with dust.

Nat and his father were out sailing—the slip at the dock was empty. Franny stood by the water. The breeze smelled of salt. Franny could still see Anna's face: the small chapped lips, eyes filled with shock at the pain that would not leave her. *I don't think I can do this,* Anna had said. *Can I let go now?* And, *will everything be here when I am gone?*

It will never be the same world without you, Franny had promised, and she had been right. Anna, her green eyes.

Franny walked in the door of the house and up the stairs to the guest room. The bed had been made, sheets pulled taut. Franny did not unmake the bed, but lay down on top of the coverlet. As soon as she closed her eyes, Franny drifted to sleep.

In her dream, the front hallway of her childhood home. Texas heat, bearing down, a new jigsaw puzzle spread before her. A tall glass of lemonade, the smell of baking earth. A slant of sunlight on the wooden floor. All the blue pieces together first, the cardboard edges rough on her fingertips. She can hold only three pieces in one small palm. Her feet are bare. Uncle Jack watches TV in her parents' living room. He is the only doctor in town, but he has taken a day off to babysit Franny on her parents' anniversary. Uncle Jack is making hamburgers for dinner, and Franny can have a Coke and a popsicle too if she stays quiet.

Dust in the driveway, Sheriff Donald. His car is white and blue. His boots are dirty, *don't walk on the rug with dirty boots.* Through the screen door his face is sad and strange. *Franny, where is your Uncle Jack?* Sheriff Donald and his boots on her puzzle. Franny sips lemonade. The ice is melted.

Donald shuts the door to the living room, but Franny can hear: *car crash, drunk driver, both of them dead.*

Uncle Jack's voice is tight: *I'll handle it. Thanks.*

Franny decides to put all the red pieces together, and then the blue. The puzzle will be a stop sign, she can see on the box. The door opens and Sheriff Donald steps on her puzzle again. *What are you making, sweetheart?* Franny does not answer. Dust in the driveway, and Franny is alone with Uncle Jack.

His hands are strong on her shoulders. *God took your Mommy and Daddy,* he says, and his voice is like an electric wire, shivering and stay away. He says, *Don't cry, Franny, they're watching you from heaven. Don't let them see you cry.* The lemonade tastes sour, and Franny drops the glass. Uncle Jack slaps her, and the slap is hard and good. He slaps her and then leans down and grabs her fiercely in his arms.

celia

The bikini arrives on Saturday in a fat brown package addressed to Mrs. Henry Mills, 2805 South First Street, Austin, TX 78701. I am sitting in my bathrobe in the front room, drinking coffee, when I see the mail truck pull up. The mailwoman's navy shorts are tight, and I can't help but think of the uncomfortable day she has ahead, what with polyester shorts and the temperature near a hundred. I make a mental note to tell Maureen that I am having positive thoughts. "I recognized at that point," I will tell Maureen, "that I would rather be me, sitting in my air-conditioned house, than that fat mailwoman in her tight shorts." Then it occurs to me that the mailwoman might have a fabulous husband at home, a husband who quite likes her shorts, and who is just waiting to jump her the minute she gets home from delivering bikinis to people like me.

I wait for the woman to head across my lawn to the house next door before I rise from the couch. Although I originally hated Henry's soft couch (I think I may have, in fact, called it "a piece of shit"), after his death I decided to keep it. It smells like Henry, for one thing, and Priscilla likes it. My mother has suggested I clean house, has even offered to buy me a snazzy living room set with her new husband's money, but I have decided that I like things the way they are. I would not tell my mother or Maureen, but there are still times that I press my face into the fabric of the couch, thinking of Henry in college, doing bong hits, even having sex with girls on the couch, playing poker, Henry in grad school, studying sheet music, Henry asleep on the ugly couch, his baby face smooth, his mouth. Sometimes I still pretend he is just away, on a trip, that he is coming home.

In the mailbox, I find an invitation from Jenny and Sean, and the bikini package. I throw away the invitation. Jenny and Sean were our best friends when Henry was alive. We met them at the dog park: when Priscilla wouldn't stop playing with their dog, Henry invited them back to our house, letting both dogs jump in the back of our truck for the ride. After that, we'd make dinner together at least once a week, drink beer in the backyard, let our dogs run each other tired. We talked about our jobs—Jenny is a programmer and Sean a history teacher—and movies we liked. We went to their wedding at the Guadalupe River Ranch, and they were the first people we called as husband and wife, from a pay phone at the Elvis Chapel.

After Henry's death, they stopped by all the time, bringing casseroles. Casseroles? We never ate them when Henry was alive. Why would I suddenly want to start eating platefuls of hot tuna? I stopped answering the door. I did not return their calls. Eventually, Sean and Jenny got the hint and let up. But they sent me an invitation to the shower for their first baby, two years ago. Then they sent me a picture of the little one.

Now, from the looks of the card in my trashcan, there's another baby on the way. Priscilla looks at me. She misses Sean and Jenny's pooch, a big mutt named Lefty. "Sorry," I tell Priscilla. There are some things I'm just not interested in seeing, and Sean and Jenny's cheery family is one of them. "They'll probably serve casserole," I tell Priscilla.

But back to the package. Both pieces of the bikini are in separate plastic bags. The magenta is even brighter than it was on the girl in the catalog. J.Crew has also included a pamphlet of new items and a coupon for five dollars off my next purchase. Priscilla has taken my spot on the couch, and she moves grumpily to the side when I sit back down. I open the pamphlet and sink into the lives in front of me: there I am, frolicking on a New England island, eating corn and crab, sitting on some lanky boy's lap, my feet in the sand.

Why not do a Texas catalog? Sweaty teens making out by Barton Springs, adorable blondes drinking margaritas and eating nachos, snotty teachers microwaving Hot Pocket sandwiches in the teachers' lounge? I think about what my personal J.Crew catalog would look like: lonely young woman talking to her dog while modeling madras culottes, librarian shelving books in an eggplant-colored tankini and wedge heels. I start to laugh, and Priscilla looks at me with pity. Maureen would not be pleased with this scenario.

I go into the bedroom to try on the bikini. Under my robe, I am wearing one of Henry's Grateful Dead T-shirts. It was one of his greatest unhappinesses that he never took me to a Dead show. We planned on driving out to California or Kentucky, but work always got in the way, and then Henry was gone, and Jerry, too. I still play Henry's bootleg tapes. His favorite show was in Oregon, in August of 1988. He would play the last song, "Knocking on Heaven's Door," on the stereo. He would lie down on the floor and close his eyes. The dog would lie beside him, and sometimes I would, too.

The bikini fits pretty damn well. I've lost weight in the last five years, which I tell my mother is one plus side of having your husband gunned down. Eating together had been a big thing for us, and I haven't gotten the hang of liking food again since Henry's death. I eat because I don't like the dizzy feeling I get when I forget to eat. I have a cabinet of vitamins and energy shakes, which are easier than dealing with a fork and knife.

I am modeling the bikini for Priscilla when the phone rings. It's been a while since reporters have called me, so I have started to answer the phone again. If it isn't my mother, it is my mother-in-law. "What are you doing, sweetie?" It is my mother.

"Trying on my new bikini," I say.

"Oh!" she says, thrilled. "The J.Crew?"

"Yup."

"Does it look fabulous?" I look at myself in the mirror,

bones and old muscles and circles carved underneath my eyes. My skin is the color of chalk. Priscilla looks at me, her head cocked.

"Yes," I say, "it does."

"Good," says my mother. "Sweetie?" she says. "Have you read the paper today?"

"No, why?"

"Oh, honey, I hate to have to tell you."

"What?" My stomach doesn't even sink anymore when people say things like this to me. It is as if my stomach is already sunk down as far as it will go, all of the time.

"They're executing one of them. Jackie something?"

"Ford," I say.

"Yes. I hope…" She pauses. "I hope this doesn't stir things up for you," says my mother. I don't say anything. "When is Henry's…when is Karen…um," says my mother.

"August twenty-fifth," I say. The execution will be held in Huntsville. Until then, Karen Lowens lives on Death Row in Mountain View Unit in Gatestown, which is about two hours from my house.

"How are you feeling about it all?"

"I don't want to talk about it."

"Well, call me, if you need anything," says my mother, trying her best over the miles. She lives in Wisconsin, where I am from.

"I will."

I hang up the phone, and there I am: a widow, in the kitchen, in a magenta bikini.

karen

Sharleen is moaning, and she won't stop. When the guard comes to wake them, Tiffany says, "For heaven's sake, see what's the matter with the Satan Killer." It is a strip search day, and they stand outside their cells in their underwear. They watch while the guards try to wake Sharleen, who tosses her head back and forth.

"It's like *The Exorcist!*" says Jackie.

Finally, Sharleen opens her eyes and spits at the guards. "I am allowed to dream," she screams, as they drag her off to isolation. "I am allowed to dream!"

"What a total freak show," says Tiffany.

The television comes on in a blaze of color and sound. Karen has been having hot flashes for days, waking feverish, covered in sweat.

They turn on the radio at eight a.m. The Texas Department of Criminal Justice does not allow phone calls: no one can call a prisoner, and a prisoner cannot call anyone. Luckily, a radio station in Waco broadcasts "Words Through Walls." People from the real world can call the radio show and give messages to prisoners. The host is Gerald Jones. Tiffany's husband calls first, as always. "Hi, Gerald," he says. Tiffany clasps her hands at the sound of his voice. She has been doing extra sit-ups all week in preparation for Dan's visit, as if he will be able to tell, underneath her jumpsuit, that her stomach is flat and strong. She will not be allowed to touch Dan, has not touched him since she entered Mountain View. Death Row inmates cannot touch anyone outside the prison, from the day they are sentenced until they are dead.

"Dan, good morning to you," says Gerald, "and do you have a message today?"

"I'm on my way to go see my baby, Tiffany," says Dan, "and wanted her to know I'd be a few minutes late—I've got to pick up a present."

"Lucky lady. Dan, anything else?"

"Yes. If anyone has any information about the terrible murder of my girls—anything that can help free my innocent wife, please, please call 1-800-FREETIF. 1-800-FREETIF."

Tiffany's color is high. "He really loves you," says Veronica. "I can tell." She looks down at her wrinkled hands. "I want a cigarette," she says.

"I wish someone would call for me," says Jackie.

"Somebody will, hon," says Veronica. This is a lie.

Tiffany spends all morning getting ready. She ties her hair up, then lets it back down. "I'm so nervous!" she says, and she rubs lotion into her elbows and hands. She is ready by nine, but visiting hours don't start until eleven.

Each Death Row inmate is allowed one visit a week. Regular inmates have visitors on the weekdays, and Death Row inmates have visitors on the weekends. Tiffany's husband has come every Saturday for two years. He brings her books and buys her Orange Crush from the soda machine. He cannot hand the sodas to his wife; he puts quarters in the machine, hands the can to a guard, and the guard gives the sweet drink to Tiffany. Dan has quit his job to free Tiffany.

Veronica will have a visitor, too: her new boyfriend. Jimmy Quinton, a plumber, started writing Veronica after seeing a show about her on television. He wrote that he thought she was misunderstood and beautiful. They have fallen in love. He writes silly letters to Veronica, and she reads them out loud sometimes. He writes about the people he works for, strange items stuck in the drain, for example, and he says how much he loves Veronica, and how he knows she is innocent. Karen is glad that someone loves Veronica, but it's pretty clear that Veronica is not innocent. They found cyanide in every dead husband.

At eleven on the dot, just as "Montel" is starting ("Teens With Attitude Confront Their Mothers"), a guard bangs on the metal door that separates them from the general inmates. "Tiffany," he says.

Tiffany jumps up, holding out her arms. As the guard cuffs her wrists and ankles, locks the metal chain connecting them, Tiffany looks over her shoulder to Veronica. "See you out there," she says. As she is led out, she looks at the floor and smiles, practically dancing.

A few minutes later, a guard calls, "Veronica!" and Veronica runs her palms over her hair before the guard shackles her and leads her off. Though she does not smile— she has been here too long to betray emotion—her eyes are shining.

Jackie kicks at the bars of her cell. "Fuck," she says.

Nobody ever comes to see Karen either. She has not had a visitor in over a year. "Want to play cards?" Jackie says. Karen shakes her head. "Fuck you, then," says Jackie.

After lunch (a piece of plastic cheese and mayonnaise on stale bread, an apple), Karen begins to feel nauseated. When she throws up in the toilet in her cell, Jackie yells to the guards in the chute, "She's sick! She needs a doctor."

Guards cuff Karen's arms and legs and take her down the hallway to Dr. Wren. Karen's chains sing as she walks. She has to go past the others, and Karen closes her eyes. As the door to the general population slides open, the noise is deafening. Metal against metal, screaming voices: *Highway Honey! Highway Honey! Highway Honey!* Karen cannot close her ears. If she hums, it does not even mar the sound. *Highway Honey! Highway Honey!*

The guards' hands are tight on her arm. Some of the women try to befriend guards, but not Karen. Karen does not want friends. Any connection, any tiny strand, will bind her to this world.

Finally, they turn the corner to the Medical Center.

Karen is searched again, and then pushed inside. She sits on a metal bench.

The Medical Center isn't much. There's a big, flat desk with file cabinets behind it. A guard sits at the desk. The nurses do almost everything: sew up stab wounds, hand out medication, belt you into straitjackets and shoot you full of Thorazine until the doctor arrives. There are some cots, two cold examining tables, and windows that show only the dark hallway, where guards can peer in. The Center smells of rubbing alcohol. People have babies somewhere else. Dr. Wren comes every Saturday and for emergencies.

It is some time before Karen is led in to see Dr. Wren. He is an old man with kind eyes and tufts of white hair by his ears. "Karen," he says, reading off a chart as she comes in. "You're feeling badly?"

"I threw up."

Dr. Wren nods. "You're HIV-positive?" he says, as if it is a question. Karen nods. "Can you describe your symptoms?" he asks. Karen shrugs. "Do you feel tired?" says Dr. Wren.

"Yes."

"How often are you sick to your stomach?" Karen shrugs again. Dr. Wren sighs. "Once in a while, or often?" he says.

"All the time, pretty much," admits Karen.

"Let's do some blood work," says Dr. Wren. "In the meantime, let's take a look at your meds." He sounds authoritative, makes a note on a clipboard, but then his eyes widen. Karen watches him, and a flash of fear sears through her. Dr. Wren staggers, and his hand goes to his chest. He drops his clipboard on the floor. He opens his mouth but no sound comes out. Karen does not know what to do. "Dr. Wren?" she says, and when he doesn't answer, his eyes falling shut, she says again, "Dr. Wren?" and finally a scream comes from her mouth, "Dr. Wren!"

A red-haired nurse rushes in, looking at Karen with wild eyes. "What have you done?" she says, and then she falls to her knees. "Jack!" she says, "Jack, wake up!"

"I didn't do anything," says Karen.

"Get her out of here," says the nurse, her voice uneven and hoarse. "Get her the hell out of here!" the nurse cries, and the guards come and take Karen away.

Later, when Tiffany comes back from her visit and shares Dan's news from the real world, when Veronica reads a letter and Jackie shows off her sequins, Karen will finally have something to offer: the story of her afternoon, and the knowledge that Dr. Wren is named Jack.

franny

Salt, chilies, tomatoes. As soon as Franny opened her apartment door, she felt as if she were inside a Mexcian restaurant. Nat had been cooking. Franny dumped her books on the side table and called, "Nat?"

He came to the kitchen door in an apron, his hands wet. "Hi there," he said.

"Hi," said Franny.

"Where have you been?"

"There was an emergency, I..."

Nat stopped her. "Never mind," he said. "You're home. I have a romantic dinner in the works."

"Nat, I'm so sorry. Tonight is not a good night for me. I've just got to grab a quick bite and head back to the hospital."

He shook his head. "I'm making chile rellenos," he said, "to bring you back to Texas."

"We didn't eat chilies," said Franny. "We ate hamburgers at the Dairy Queen."

"Nonetheless," said Nat. He held up his palms against

her protests, and then disappeared back into the kitchen.

"Nat, listen," she said. He reappeared with a margarita glass, lined in salt.

"Drink up," he said. He held it out to her.

"Nat…"

"Take it," he said. His eyes were a warning.

"No. I have to read a stack of—"

Nat threw the glass. It rolled across the hall, spilling tequila, but did not break. "Nat," she said, "let me explain."

"No," he said, "I don't want explanations from you. I want some answers."

"Can this wait? I just—"

He grabbed her wrist and pulled her into the kitchen. On the stove, a pot simmered, and he turned off the flame. "Sit down," he said. Franny sat.

"It seems to me," said Nat, "that you no longer want to marry me."

"Nat—"

"Let me finish." He took a breath. "There was a time," said Nat, "when being with me was what you wanted. You used to come to my shows, you used to like my friends. I used to feel like we were a team. I know that your career is important to you, but I just thought…"

"What?" said Franny. "You thought what? That I would ignore my patients? What kind of a person do you think I am?"

"I didn't think our house—our home—would be filled with shit, Franny. I thought you'd leave it behind, and come home and love me."

"How can I?" said Franny. "How can I think about

dinner and margaritas? If you had any idea what I deal with every day…"

"You know, I'm sorry. I'm sorry you have to go through what you have to go through. But there has to be something left for me. You make me feel as if my life, and my problems, and my career are…"

"Trivial?" said Franny. There was a silence.

"Let me say, Franny," Nat looked at her coldly, "that if this is the life you plan to lead—all excuses, no time for me or anyone but your…your fucking sick patients—until you dry up inside and turn into a bitter old woman, well, frankly, I don't think I want to marry you."

Franny had nothing to say.

"Franny," said Nat. "Do you want to be my wife?"

The smell of chilies was making Franny dizzy, the sheer heat. She said, "I…"

"Yes or no," said Nat. He leaned against the stove, and tears filled his eyes and then ran over.

"I can't…" said Franny.

"*Yes or no!*" The bottle of tequila on the counter was half-empty.

"I don't know," said Franny.

Nat put fingers to his eyes, pressed in. After a moment, he took them away. He was crying openly now. "That's a no," he said, choking. "That's a no to me."

The phone rang once, twice, and a third time. Nat watched Franny, and she picked up the phone.

"Miss Wren?" said a voice thick with the sound of Texas. "Franny Wren?"

"Yes?" said Franny. "Who is this?"

Nat took his apron off and picked up the tequila. In six steps and a slam, he was gone.

"Franny, honey, I'm calling from the prison in Gatestown. I'm calling about your Uncle Jack."

celia

When school lets out, the library fills up. Parents drop off their kids when they need some downtime, and people come over to spend their lunch hour in the air-conditioning. Things get mixed up and turned around, and it drives me up the wall. If I had my way, I would only let two people in the library: an elderly man named Abe who comes to read the paper, and an eight-year-old boy who is saddled with the name Finnegan. Neither Abe nor Finnegan ever leaves encyclopedias in the Periodical Area or leaves books pushed open to save their places, mashing them willy-nilly with no regard for their fragile spines.

I believe there are very few respectful humans on the planet, and you can tell immediately who they are from how they act in libraries and hotel rooms. You have the people who carve their initials into library tables and who leave dirty plates in hotel rooms. I dated (not only dated, I am sorry to admit, but *slept with*) a man who would mess the sheets around on hotel beds even if he hadn't slept in them.

He would sleep in one bed (OK, *we* would sleep in one bed, and not just sleep, he was good in the sack, I'll give him that) and wake up in the morning and pull the sheets off the other bed *just because he could.* Because someone would have to make that bed, and he had paid to have both beds made. This is the same type of person who quietly (but not quietly enough—I always hear them) rips articles from library newspapers and sticks them in their pocket, or who fills in crossword puzzles or even worse *love quizzes* with complete disregard for the fact that someone else might want to know *HOW SERIOUS IS HE?* or *ARE YOU THE JEALOUS TYPE?*

But then there are people like Abe and Finnegan. People who always say hello to the librarian, even ask about her day, people who fold the newspaper when they're finished or who always put *Clifford the Big Red Dog* books back on the shelf, in alphabetical order, no less. If I could create my own perfect world, it would be me in the library with Abe and Finnegan, and Henry still alive at home.

Instead, I get busybodies like Geraldine Flat. Geraldine has not a damn thing to do since her husband got the job on the oil rig, two weeks on and two weeks off. She has money coming out of her nostrils and diddlysquat to keep her busy. (Geraldine used to be a nail technician, but quit as soon as her husband's bucks started rolling in. She went back to school to get her college degree, and began wearing miniskirts, knee-high boots, and baby T-shirts.) I would like to stick a hot poker up Geraldine's nose, but I do not share this sentiment with anyone, especially Maureen, who would certainly allude to my anger management issues.

"I gather you've been following the news about the prison," says Geraldine on Thursday, putting a stack of Harlequin romances on the checkout table and raising her eyebrow.

I stamp her books firmly with my red rubber stamp (which I love) and answer, "These are due the fifth of August, Geraldine."

"I'm against the death penalty," says Geraldine. "You know, it isn't so great to live your whole life in that prison, either, and what right do we have?" From the strident tone of Geraldine's voice, I can tell she has been planning this conversation for some time. Her words run over each other as she struggles to get them all out. I don't answer, and don't look up. I become extremely engrossed in my new copy of *Library Journal.* "What do you believe?" says Geraldine, her voice lowering, attempting to invite a tearful confession from me.

"What?"

"I said, what do you believe? About the death penalty?"

Tears fill my eyes, and I do not look up. "You know," says Geraldine, "some of us students are holding a protest this weekend over at the U. If you came and made a statement, maybe asked for mercy, you could make a real difference."

I don't answer. I do not know what to say. I am speechless. "Think about it," whispers Geraldine, placing a pink pamphlet under my nose. The pamphlet reads, "Two Wrongs Do Not Make a Right." Geraldine gathers her romance novels and leaves me at my desk.

After a moment, I stand up and smooth my skirt. I walk

to the ladies' room. I lock the door behind me and peer into the mirror. It has been five years since Henry died, and I still wear my hair long, the way he loved it. I still buy Ritz crackers at the grocery store, but I can't remember if it was me or Henry who liked them. I go to movies he would enjoy, and hike alone down the trails he loved so dearly. I live our life without him, because I don't want any life of my own.

I know that Karen Lowens' execution will never bring Henry back. I know, as well, that Karen is a fucked-up individual who has every right to live the rest of her life trying to make amends. I know that only God can take a life, that the death penalty is wrong. I know this in my bones. I also know that Henry would not want her executed.

I know all this, and yet I do not care. I hate that woman for taking everything from me and Goddamn it, I want her dead.

Maureen has told me to write a letter to Karen, to tell her how I feel. This letter is an exercise, Maureen was quick to tell me, and simply for my own well-being. It is not a letter to be mailed, but a letter to be burned, releasing some of the bitter anger that, despite my denials, I hold deep within my soul.

Back at my desk, I take a fresh legal pad from my drawer. After checking out a stack of gardening books for a man who looks like Gomer Pyle (and who, interestingly, has no dirt underneath his nails), I take a breath.

I begin with "Dear Karen," and then I stop, and cross it out. I try again: "To Ms. Lowens," and then the words come.

part two
july

karen

Needles are something they talk about in Mountain View Unit. Lethal injection is the default method of execution in the state of Texas, and everybody has an opinion. Veronica hates needles. If she had her choice, she declares, she would choose a firing squad. (Bill, Veronica's third husband, was killed with a bullet. Although he had arsenic in his body, when they finally found him under the wishing well in Veronica's yard, the coroners decided it had been the gunshot to the back of his head that had finally done him in.)

Tiffany will not discuss her own execution, but says that needles in general give her the willies. She has always hated shots, she says, and even when her girls, may they rest in peace, had to get their shots, she would close her eyes. Needles, she says, are gross.

Jackie wants the needle. It won't hurt, she says, and she's always loved the drugs you get at the dentist. Those big pink pills? Vicodin, like after you get teeth pulled, good old Uncle Vikey. She loves that stuff. It's like getting taken down a warm river, she says—bring it on. She has three weeks until her execution.

Karen wants to go cleanly, and without pain. She wants to slip into silence. Jackie says that if quiet is what she wants, she should go for the needle. Sharleen does not join them on the patio while they eat breakfast and talk. There isn't a chair for her, anyway. Not yet.

Thursday is Karen's birthday. She is twenty-nine, and has been on Death Row for five years. She feels a hundred years old.

Karen was born in Uvalde, Texas, a tiny town near San Antonio where there weren't many black people. Her mother spent her nights in the city, turning tricks and shooting whatever she could find into her arm. When Karen's mother was pregnant, she had settled down for a while, living with Karen's grandmother in the trailer in Uvalde, but soon after Karen was born, her mother took off for the high life of the city again. She would come to town once in a while, take Karen for ice cream cones. When Karen was twelve, her grandmother died and her mother started selling Karen to men, bringing them to the trailer and then bringing Karen to the city.

When Karen's mother died (beaten to death, one cheekbone snapped), Karen did not know how to feel. There was relief, but there was also loneliness. Karen no longer had a home. She left Uvalde for good when she was fifteen. Once, when she was small, her grandmother made Apple Brown Betty for her birthday.

◆ ◆ ◆

Since she is sick, the guards do not make Karen work. She lies on her cot. If she looks to the right of her cell, she can just see the others sewing in the cage. They sit behind the machines, underneath the dolls. They are not supposed to talk, but they whisper occasionally, and touch each other's arms and hands, pressing skin to skin. On top of the television, there is a photograph from their Christmas party. They had made invitations for each other, and the guard had taken the invitations and delivered them the next day, like mail, like real invitations. In the picture, their arms are around each other, and they are smiling: Highway Honey, Black Widow, Baby Killer, and the Hairdresser of Death (in a Santa hat).

By afternoon, Karen is so dizzy that she falls when she tries to make it to the table for lunch. Two guards take her to the Medical Center. A nurse slides a needle in her arm. Her nausea subsides, and her limbs feel heavy. She is given her meds with a cup of water. She does not ask what has happened to Dr. Wren, and no one tells her.

Lying on a cot in the Medical Center, Karen thinks of Ellen. She can see Ellen in her mind: the curly thick hair, the wide smile. The tummy, just the tiniest bit soft, before she started using again and her stomach sank into her hipbones. Ellen. She was the only one who had loved Karen, but she loved her the most when they had money. That was why Karen turned tricks, why she went out on the road, thumbing from rest stop to rest stop, getting it stuck in her for a few dollars, a twenty, a ten. For Ellen, it was all for Ellen, to come home to their room at the Hi-D-Ho Motel with beer and clothes, cash for Ellen's smack.

Ellen had cried on her birthday. She cried because Karen had nothing to give her. Karen had worked for five days on the highway to come home with enough money for the previous month's rent and for beer. "You don't love me," Ellen said. "You didn't even bring me a birthday present." And she put her clothes in a suitcase, slammed it shut, her eyes bright with the heroin.

Karen begged her not to leave. "I'll get you a present," said Karen, "I promise I will, please," and finally Ellen was soothed. Karen tucked her into bed, turned on the television, left Ellen the beer. And after four nights with no sleep, she went out again onto the highway.

The first car that slowed had two men in it, and Karen kept walking. Her jeans were dirty and her shirt smelled of sweat, but she was skinny then and wore bright lipstick and push-up bras. The second car was a white Toyota with a heavy man. Karen got in.

At the Evergreen Rest Stop, she let him stick it in her. He didn't want to get muddy, so he laid a blanket on the ground. He gave her a twenty—she always made them pay first. He gave her some whiskey to drink, pretended like it was a date, and then he stuck it in her. He was fat and heaving, his stomach white and soft and Karen thought about Ellen, her skin, her strawberry lotion, and the man pumped away. Finally he finished, got off her, and went to the car. Karen pulled her jeans on, the fabric rough on her hips. Was a twenty enough to go home? She could buy Ellen some chocolates with a twenty, or some flowers at the Circle-K. A bottle of champagne? She saw the man rummaging in his glove compartment.

"You can just leave me here," Karen said, standing, brushing a twig from her hair. The man moved toward her, his feet making crunching sounds in the grass. Karen knelt to fold up the blanket. She would hitch a ride home. The flowers would buy her another week with Ellen. Another day, at least. She needed sweet sleep.

When the man's fist hit her cheek, it was a complete surprise. The gun was in his hand, and the force knocked her to the ground. He straddled her. "Give me my money back, whore," he said, his lip curling. Karen put her hand to her cheek. There was blood. The man pressed the gun to her temple.

"In my jeans," said Karen. Her voice was surprisingly even.

He heaved off her, watched her put her hand into her pocket. She kicked him in the groin as hard as she could, her bony knee in the softest flesh. He cried out, loosened his hold on the gun, and she grabbed it. She shot him in the face, she shot him in the heart. It was too much. It was enough. She shot him again and again and then she took the ring from his finger and she ran.

Ellen was sitting up in bed, playing solitaire. "What happened?" she said, when Karen arrived.

"Nothing."

Karen went into the bathroom, rinsed her clothes. There was not too much blood on them. She stood under a hot shower and lathered herself with the cheap motel soap.

When she climbed into bed, the sheets smelled like Ellen. Karen put her head on Ellen's belly, hiding the throbbing, bruised cheek. "I love you," she said.

"I know," said Ellen. Her fingers played with Karen's hair.

"Happy birthday," said Karen. She opened her hand.

"A ring!" said Ellen, "It's gold! Where did you get it?"

"Is it good?" said Karen.

Ellen slipped it on her finger. It was huge, and it shone in the lamplight. "It's perfect," she said. The next day, she would buy a length of leather cord and wear the ring around her neck, nestled between her clavicle bones.

Karen had closed her eyes then, but before she drifted into the deepest sleep, she thought, *This is it. The beginning of the end.*

When Karen gets back to her cell from the Medical Center, the area around the patio is strewn with toilet paper. There are buckets filled with Tang and broken-up candy bars arranged on paper plates. There are tubs of ice cream, melting quickly. (They can order ice cream from the commissary, but have to eat it right away: they have no refrigerator, let alone a freezer.) In the middle of the table is a honeybun, a sliver of cardboard made to look like a candle stuck deep in its frosting. There is also a piece of paper.

Karen unfolds the paper. It says, "Happy Birthday from The Girls" in fancy writing, and then there is a picture of a daisy. Karen turns around, and they are all looking at her. Tiffany claps her hands. She is smiling so widely that Karen can't help but smile too. Even Jackie has stopped scowling.

Veronica points with a long fingernail. "I drew the card," she says. Sharleen is watching from her cell, standing with her hands around the bars. A few steps, and she could join them. Karen feels a welling inside her, hot and sweet. She leans in, holds her arms out, and for a moment, they hold each other, the girls.

franny

Instead of getting married, Franny flew to Waco, Texas. She felt like a bad country song. She left JFK, an airport filled with sleek women dressed in black, and arrived in Waco surrounded by men in Stetson hats. She leaned against the wall of the airport under a poster of a longhorn bull and watched the bags turn lazily on the carousel: camouflage duffel, red Samsonite suitcase, cardboard box tied with twine. There was a poster on the wall that read "Visit Gatestown: The Spur Capital of the World!"

Finally, Franny's bag came around, and she grabbed it and headed outside. The electric door slid open and the heat seared Franny's lungs. The air was swampy heat, a marshy bath. The smell was barbecue smoke, truck exhaust, cow manure, and dust. It was scorched earth and cheap beer. Stars, sausage, ham sandwiches, lemonade, padded bras, sweaty pantyhose, hairspray, gum, condoms like slippery fish on her fingers.

She was back in Texas, and felt as if she had never left.

Evenings with Uncle Jack in front of the TV, chicken pot pies, fish sticks, ketchup, losing her virginity to Joey Ullins in the bed of his Toyota pickup. The night Sheriff Donald found her with Joey, sixteen years old and half-undressed under the starry sky. The Sheriff brought Franny home to Uncle Jack. She smelled of sex and was hot with shame.

Uncle Jack sent her away to boarding school the following year. After that, Franny rarely came home. She spent the school years in Connecticut, going to sleep-away camp and then to Cape Cod in the summers. She had forgotten the stifling heat. She struggled for breath, and lifted her hand for a cab.

"First visit to Texas?" said the driver, a dark man with bushy nose hair, as she collapsed into the cab.

"Please," said Franny, "turn on the air-conditioning." The man laughed. He was covered with a thin sheen of sweat. He rolled up his window, and in a few minutes Franny could breathe. She gave the man the hospital's address.

As the ribbon of road unfolded before her, Franny tried to remember the last conversation she had had with Uncle Jack. For years, they spoke every Sunday evening, but after Franny moved in with Nat, the phone calls became less frequent.

When Uncle Jack finally visited New York, things had not gone well. Franny winced when she remembered Nat's expression, looking Uncle Jack over, from his hat to his boots. Nat had even pulled Franny aside and told her "the doc" might want to change if they were really going to go out to dinner. "I'm just looking out," Nat had said. "And he's my size, so if he wants to borrow something…"

Franny had told Nat to go to hell, but then, as Uncle Jack pulled a jacket over his worn denim shirt and leaned over to wipe his boots (the good leather ones), she saw him suddenly through new eyes: a country bumpkin, a man out of a Wynonna Judd video. And she had looked up and met Nat's gaze, realizing how Nat had seen Uncle Jack from the beginning, how he must see Franny at times. Franny could cry now thinking about it. She had asked Uncle Jack into the kitchen and had suggested that her proud uncle, a doctor, the man who had raised her, might want to change his clothes. Franny had half-hoped he'd laugh at her, something to bring her back to herself, but he just shook his head. He went into the bedroom and put on the suit Nat had laid out for him. Brooks Brothers.

As soon as Franny walked inside the Waco hospital, the cold air on her skin like water, she felt that something was wrong. It was in the hollow sound of her footsteps, the nervous glance of the nurse when she asked for Uncle Jack's room. Even as she walked down the gleaming hallway, she thought, *he's gone.* She felt Uncle Jack's absence from the world in the pit of her stomach. And she was right.

"He tried to hold on for you, Fran. It was his heart gave out," said the man standing next to the empty bed. Franny blinked. She recognized the man as a friend of Uncle Jack's. His name was Ed. "You look great," he added, lamely.

"Thanks," said Franny.

"Do you want to see him?" asked a woman standing to Ed's right. She was plump, with long reddish hair. She wore gray slacks and a pink cotton cardigan, and her eyes were teary. Franny nodded, and the woman reached into her pink purse and pulled out a business card. She gave it to Franny. Franny knew the address on the card; it was where her parents' funeral had been. "I'm Deborah," said the woman, pressing her fingers into Franny's palm.

Stay focused, Franny told herself. "What was the time of death?" she asked.

Ed looked at her strangely, but said, "Early this morning, four or five."

She had been at the airport then, checking the bag she had frantically packed for what she thought might be a long visit.

"Fran?" said Ed, reaching into the pocket of his jeans.

"Yes?"

"These are his keys."

"Yes. Of course." Franny watched as Ed opened his fist, and she took the familiar keychain from it, a silver loop.

"Do you want a ride? Jack's car, it's at the prison. Mountain View Unit."

"Thanks," said Franny. The woman named Deborah still stood at the foot of the bed, staring. The hospital had re-made the bed. The sheets were tight, and Franny reached out to feel the cool fabric against her fingers.

"What are you doing?" said Deborah.

"Nothing," said Franny.

Ed's car was large and smelled of cigars. "Well, it's been some time," he said. "What, ten years since you've been home?"

Franny didn't answer, and Ed fell silent. He turned on

the radio, and the country song was faintly familiar. They drove slowly along the road, flat trees on either side of them. They came to Gatestown, passed the cemetery where Franny's parents were buried, and then the prison complexes, and Main Street. On Fourth, Ed took a left, and the house came into view.

The house. There was the tree Franny had fallen from, breaking her ankle, her cry bringing Uncle Jack running with his medical kit, holding her ankle still and wrapping it with cold, wet plaster strips. The lawn where Franny had laid out elaborate tea parties and then invited Uncle Jack, who would fold his long legs awkwardly and sip from the tiny cups. The front step where they sat in the evenings, Uncle Jack with his pipe and Franny with her glass of lemonade. Franny had been Uncle Jack's girl for so long that she didn't know what she was supposed to be, now that he was gone.

The house looked better than Franny had remembered; Uncle Jack had always taken care of the lawn, but now there were flowers in the window boxes, and the front door was newly painted. "Well, you know I'm here, honey," said Ed, as he eased the car to a stop.

"Yes," said Franny. She looked sideways at Ed, his solid frame, and she suddenly wanted to throw her arms around him. But she did not.

"Well, thank you," said Franny. "Thank you, Ed."

"How about I have Joanne bring over some food for you?"

"No, thank you," said Franny, "I'm fine. I'll go over to the funeral home tomorrow."

"Well, honey, I don't think you should be alone just now," said Ed, but Franny was already out of the car, and halfway to the house.

How easily the key slid in the door. Franny remembered sneaking into the house after lying in the grass with Joey Ullins until nearly dawn, her lips and chin chafed by kisses, her key fumbling in this very lock. Uncle Jack had been awake, of course, sitting in the living room and fixing her with a disappointed stare. Until the last night, when the disappointment had turned to anger.

Some of the furniture had been moved around—the wing chairs had been replaced with a couch, and the television no longer blocked the fireplace—but after ten years, the smell was the same: pipe tobacco, Old Spice, and pine needles. Franny sighed and stepped across the threshold. She dropped her bag on the floor, and walked slowly up the stairs to her room.

Her room was not the same. Her bed was there, and her bureau, and the green rug with fish on it that she had begged so doggedly for one Christmas. But her posters were gone, and there was a large desk in the room that was covered with scraps of cloth. Uncle Jack, sewing? Franny lay down on her bed, the familiar bedsprings folding around her bones, and she waited for the sorrow to come.

Pictures flashed in her mind: Anna reading in her hospital bed, Uncle Jack shaving in the bathroom mirror. Franny sat up. There was no point to this.

She couldn't find any liquor in the house, which was strange. Uncle Jack had always liked his Scotch, but the cabinets were empty. In the refrigerator, there was diet soda, Tab, which was another mystery. Franny opened the front door. The edge of the heat had faded now that the sun had set, and she began to walk briskly. Eventually Franny came upon an old apartment building that had been converted into a motel, the Gatestown Motor Inn. She sighed. It looked as if the market for housing visitors to the prison was growing faster than Gatestown's population.

She walked into the lobby, and the smell of cigarette smoke raised her hopes that there was a bar. At the front desk, an old lady sat knitting.

"Is there a bar in this motel?" asked Franny.

The woman looked up. "There's a lounge," she said, pointing to a frosted-glass door.

The air in the lounge was smoky and wet. A woman in a muumuu played piano, a martini balanced on the piano bench beside her. A few men in suits drunkenly watched Franny as she walked in. She sat on an orange barstool.

"Can I help you?" The bartender was young, blond, skinny. His nametag said, "Hello! I'm FRED."

"Scotch on the rocks," said Franny.

Fred poured the drink. "You in town long?" he said.

"Yes," said Franny.

"Here for the execution?" He said this in the same blasé tone, and Franny looked up at him. He pointed to the men at the other tables. "That's why they're all here. The Hairdresser of Death."

"Sorry?"

"You don't know about her?" Fred pulled a newspaper

out from under the bar. He folded it back to show a grainy picture of a tired-looking woman. "Killed her whole family," said Fred.

"Wow."

"That's nothing. We've got some real sickos up there." Franny didn't answer, didn't even nod. She wanted the bartender to be quiet. "I'm gonna be a prison guard," he said. He was a type familiar to Franny. She had gone to school with dozens of beefy boys who were likely guards now. It was one of the few jobs in town. Franny played with her cocktail napkin, and calculated how fast she could finish her drink and leave. Ten minutes, she thought, maybe five. "You okay, lady?" said Fred. Franny nodded. She drained the Scotch and pulled a five from her wallet. As she made her way out of the bar, the piano player sang, "I get no kick from champagne!"

Back at the house, the phone was ringing. Franny picked it up. "Honey?" said Nat. "How is he?"

"He's dead."

"Oh God, Fran. I'm getting the next plane."

"No," said Franny.

"What do you mean? You need me."

"Nat, I don't want you." Franny said the words without even thinking, but once they were spoken, she realized they were true.

"What?"

"I don't want you…here. I don't want it. I'm sorry."

There was a silence. "I'm going to let you go now," said

Nat, his voice even with anger. "I'm very sorry about your Uncle Jack, and I'm going to call you tomorrow."

"Goodbye," said Franny, and she hung up the phone and pulled the plug from the wall.

She walked up the stairs again and paused at the door of Uncle Jack's room. There was the bed she had once climbed into when she was scared or lonely. There was a time when she had been terrified of an imaginary group of people who would come at night and lock everyone in their basements. One night, in Uncle Jack's bed again, Franny had told him about her terrible fear. "Baby Doll," he had said, his hand on her head, pushing her hair behind her ears, "we don't have a basement." In that moment, Franny had known that he could save the world.

She walked down the hall to her old bedroom, and lay down, staring at the ceiling. The crack had been repaired, but there was still a water stain in the left corner. She began to remember her last conversation with Uncle Jack. He had called on a Sunday a few months ago, and she had been running out the door to taste wedding cakes with Nat. "I just want to know how things are going, Baby Doll," Uncle Jack had said. "It gets lonely here, nighttimes. I'd like a nice long chat one of these days."

"I'll call you back," Franny had said, thinking of sugar frosting and Italian cream cake. "I promise," she said, but she never called. Had she told Uncle Jack she loved him? Had she ever thanked him for being a mother and a father and a friend? Franny made herself say it out loud: *Uncle Jack is dead.*

celia

The post office in my neighborhood is a squat building made of concrete. Inside, three fabulous men process mail: Claudel, a tall black man with heavy eyelids and a ready smile; Rick, a man I would call jolly—it certainly describes him—but for the fact that he is fat, and everyone always calls fat people jolly, and so very few of them really are; and Joe, a wiry blond who has a very foul mouth and doesn't mind using it. (Joe is a bit pudgy, too, but he is *by no means* jolly.) In truth, I like Claudel the best, because he always asks me how I'm doing, and he really seems to care. Also, he's sexy.

So I went to mail my letter. I even bought a to-go cup of Starbucks for the occasion. I love the cardboard cup at Starbucks, and I love the little corrugated cardboard sleeve. The whole package just makes me feel like I'm going places. With one of those cups of coffee in my hand, I feel as if I'm on "Law & Order," rushing to the rescue in black leather boots. But Starbucks is expensive. It's really a ripoff. I only allow myself a cup on special occasions—for example mailing a letter to a murderess.

There were many people in line ahead of me at the South Austin Post Office and the excessive caffeine in my Starbucks was starting to make me nervous and paranoid. What do they put in that coffee? I'd really like to know. I have a sneaking suspicion there's something illegal in there, and at the prices they charge, there should be.

The people in line started chatting, as will sometimes happen in cramped spaces like buses when the driver gets off to go to the bathroom leaving you stranded at some curb, and (I have heard) submarines. There was one woman with a large package that, she announced, was candy for her niece at summer camp. Holding up an enormous overnight envelope, a boy confided he was sending his first novel to a literary agent. Like we were in a group therapy session, a man piped in that he was mailing a book about plants to his mother in Topeka; a tween said she was mailing a letter to the Spice Girls Fan Club (I have read about these "tweens" in *Time Magazine*, these twelve- to fourteen-year-olds who are running our economy); a girl bashfully admitted she was sending a love letter to her boyfriend, home for the summer in Maine. "I promised I'd write every day," said the girl, blushing. "But I ran out of stamps."

I'd been smiling away, listening to everyone's confessions, nodding encouragement, and when the silence fell, they looked to me. The line still had quite a way to go. I lifted my gaze to the posters of stamps on the wall. I pretended to be deeply interested in the Marilyn Monroe Collector's Edition Stamp Set.

"How about you?" said the wannabe novelist, his glasses perched on the end of his nose. "What's up with your letter?"

First of all, it's illegal to ask questions like that. I'm sorry, but it is. Secondly, I could see his little brain turning: *Wow, is this going to be a great short story! I'll call it "At the Post Office," or "Fed-Exing My Heart."* I clutched my envelope.

"Uh," I said. The group-therapy post office line looked at me expectantly. The candy lady hefted her package to her hip. Topeka man raised his eyebrows encouragingly.

I decided to play it straight. (This was when my sanity began to come into question. Maureen would have told me I could have demurely mentioned "a pen pal" and let the matter rest. But I did not.) "Well," I said, holding up the letter, which was neatly packaged in a clean white envelope, the kind I use to send student loan checks and bank deposits, "I wrote a letter to the woman who murdered my husband. She's on Death Row."

There was silence. The candy woman's face drained, and she turned away from me. She had a sweat stain on her back, between her shoulder blades. Everyone looked away, except the eager novelist, who perked up. "What did you write to her?" he asked.

"None of your fucking business," I said. Then I said, "Just kidding."

He looked sad. "I'm sorry," he said. He couldn't have been more than twenty, with his guileless expression and pretentious little haircut.

"I just told her how angry I was," I said. "I told her about Henry." The boy listened quietly. "I told her how

Henry used to—" I said, and then I felt something hot in my throat. "How he used to chase the dog around on all fours," I said. "How he used to pretend to talk to the dog, and tell her to make us coffee and bring it to us in bed."

I have never heard a post office so quiet. The shuffling, the tossing, the stuffing, the stamping, it all fell silent. "Hey," said Claudel, who had finally noticed us. "Leave Celia alone!"

Instead of crying, I turned, and I left.

The boy with the novel ran after me. In the parking lot, he grabbed my arm. "Could I—do you want some coffee?" he said. I opened my mouth, but nothing came out. The boy dropped his novel on the ground. I held my letter. He took me in his arms, and I cried.

karen

"**K**aren," says Rick Underwood, "what's this about not appealing?"

Karen lifts her shoulders. Her hands and feet are shackled. Rick looks even more tired than usual. He looks old. When Rick talks, spittle hits the glass between them. "Karen," he says, as if repeating her name will change things, "I don't understand."

"I'm tired," Karen says.

"You're tired?" Rick puts his thumb and forefinger between his eyebrows and presses. His nails are bitten to the quick. *Ouch*, thinks Karen. "Karen," he says again, "if you do not appeal, you will be executed on August twenty-fifth." He looks at her pleadingly. She knows that this is the only power she has: she can decide to stop fighting.

"Rick," she says, "I'm so tired."

"You look terrible. Are they giving you anything?"

Karen shakes her head. "The doctor's gone."

"Well, for fuck's sake," says Rick, balling his fists. "I want you to think hard about appealing. You don't have much time. I suppose you know that. In the meantime, I'll get you a doctor." He tugs on his ill-fitting jacket. "Where the hell is Dr. Wren?" he mutters, shaking his head. "Oh," he says, before leaving, "here."

It is a plain white bag. Inside it, an origami book and colorful squares of paper.

When Karen was first arrested, Rick visited her in jail. She was still crazy with grief, and could not believe that Ellen had turned her in. Karen had been waked in the middle of the night at the Hi-D-Ho Motel and dragged outside in a T-shirt and underwear, her hair wild and her eyes blinded by the flashing police lights. They handcuffed her and put her in the police car. Karen cried, "Ellen!" looking out the window of the car, her eyes clouded with tears.

But Ellen did not answer. She was standing in the doorway of the motel room, looking down at the floor, her arms crossed over her chest. She did not look up as the police drove Karen away.

Karen was read her rights: *multiple murders, roadside prostitution, right to remain silent.* They told her to confess, slamming fists on the metal table. She did not speak. She needed Ellen, and Ellen needed her. The police told her, their growling voices, that Ellen had called her in. It was not true. It could not be true. Ellen wore on her own body the ring from the first, the necklace from the third, the pinkie ring from...was it the sixth or seventh? Ellen drank the beer, ate the Stouffer's dinners, shot the men's money into her arm. It could not be true. It was not true.

Karen was in a cell with other women (and had just begun to understand the noise of the prison, the way it cut into you and would not let you rest) when Rick came with a guard to the door. "Karen Lowens," the guard said, his voice flat. Karen stood (the other women arguing, talking, *who you think you are bitch fucking bitch* and on and on and never being quiet never never just shutting their goddamn mouths) and the guard unlocked the door and let her through.

"I'm Rick Underwood," said the man with the crazy black hair and the eyes like a bird, darting. He held out his hand, and when Karen touched it, wrapped her fingers around, he did not wince or pull away. His fingers were firm; they gripped Karen's hand, squeezed some strength into her. Rick and Karen went into one of the concrete rooms and Rick gave her a cigarette, lit it for her. His voice was slow and drawling, deep Texas, his manners a gentleman's.

"You're in a pile of trouble," he told her. "Your girlfriend called the cops on you."

"No," said Karen. "That's a lie."

"Honey, I wish it was. She called the cops and she told them everything. They've got the jewelry."

"The jewelry?" Karen's voice wavered.

"Let's see," said Rick, reading off his notes, "one large gold wedding band, inscribed 'Forever Mary.' One gold chain. One pinkie ring with diamond chips. You want me to go on?"

"No," said Karen. She was silent for a moment, breathless, as if she'd been punched in the gut. "Can I—can I see her?"

"Why?"

"I need to see her."

"I'll see what I can do." Rick put out his cigarette in the plastic ashtray that said "Property of Texas." He leaned back, lifted his arms, and laced his fingers behind his head. There were two wet spots on his shirt under his arms. "So, what's the story?" said Rick.

Karen looked at her fingers, did not speak. She had a hangnail on her right hand, and started to pick it, drawing blood.

"Karen, I'm not here for my own benefit. They'll put you to death. Did you kill these men?"

"Yes."

"Why?"

Karen looked into his sharp eyes, and began the story. She told him everything. Ellen's curls, the first time they had made love after drinking too much beer at Ed's Saloon, their movements slow and sweet. The heroin, and the way Ellen would cry and say that Karen didn't love her. Ellen, packing her things in the blue suitcase and slamming out the door. The joy on Ellen's face when Karen came home with flowers, beer, sandwiches, money. The men at the rest stops and the parks, the creased twenties, dirty tens. The spread-out blankets, the smell of shit from the woods mixed with the smell of dirt, the hot pricks, rubbing on her dry insides. And then the one she killed. The first one, his gun hitting her cheekbone. The one who cut her, stuck a knife inside her, blood on his pinkie ring. The one who punched her black and blue until she pulled the gun.

"How many?"

I don't remember, I don't remember.

And the last night, when the man hadn't died, lying down on the ground like the rest of them. Somewhere, some park in Austin. The man with the black van and the flannel shirt who had fucked her up the ass until she threw up and had then kept pounding, pushing her face down. He had smelled sour, the sweat, old beer on his skin. After she had taken the gun from her coat and shot blindly to make him stop, the man had run from Karen. His shoulder bleeding, a red blossom growing on the flannel shirt. He ran and Karen ran after him.

The power washed over her.

"The power?" said Rick.

The power, yes. The man ran quickly, despite the shot. He reached his van, but his keys were in his pants, and his pants were in the woods.

He ran from the rest stop, heading to a bright building, a 7-Eleven. Karen ran after him. It happened so quickly: the man, yelling at the cashier, and Karen aiming the gun. She shot him in the back, and then the cashier, a thin man she barely saw. But it wasn't over. The neon lights of the store, the rows of chips and candy, the radio so loud in her ears, louder than her own thumping heart. She had to get back to Ellen. "At least two hundred dollars," Ellen had said.

Karen shot the cash register. She pulled the money,

stuffed it in her pockets, knew she had only seconds to get back to the motel and to Ellen. The radio, the radio and then the door swung open. It was a white man, with dark hair and a smile that went cold as he looked around him. He wore a T-shirt that said "Elvis Lives." He looked at Karen and began to shake his head and bring his hands up, as if they could save him, as if they made any difference and he was in between Karen and the door and she shot him and she shot him until he fell down and the path was clear.

But she did not leave. The man's eyes went to Karen, and she held her breath. She watched him open his mouth. "I'm going to die," the man said, but it was a question. Karen held the gun with one hand, and put the other to her mouth. She watched him go. He said something before he died, something that made no sense to Karen.

"No, Celia," he said. And then he was dead.

She had never seen one pass over before. She had shot the men and left them in the shadows. She bent down, touched the man on the head, it wasn't even real. She left. She ran to the motel, and to Ellen, her feet slapping the road like words.

Rick had taken notes as she had talked. The guard in the corner had snorted and made sounds of disbelief. But Rick listened, wrote in his careful hand, looked up, looked right at Karen. When she was done, tears covering her cheeks, he stood and put his hand on hers. "I'll do everything I can," he said.

"Ellen," said Karen. "Can I see her, please?"

"I'll do everything I can," said Rick again.

Ellen visited, once. They took Karen from her cell without telling her where she was going, without giving her a chance to brush her hair. Ellen sat behind the glass, straight-backed in a wooden chair, her face still, her lips thin and tight. She picked up the phone without looking at Karen. Her nails were manicured.

"Ellen," said Karen, "Ellen, I love you. Do you love me?"

"Yes," said Ellen. "Of course I do."

"Really?" Karen held the receiver so tightly that her knuckles were white. Her breathing was shallow and fast. Ellen did not want to be there, and Karen did not want to see it, the fear on Ellen's face. "Did you...did you do this? Did you call the police?"

"I didn't know what to do," said Ellen. Her voice was stiff, starched.

"What?"

"When I found out you had killed people, I was afraid."

"Ellen, you always knew! How could you...why did you..."

"I don't know what you're talking about," said Ellen. Before the police, Ellen had gone to visit her parents in Dallas. They had put her up to this.

"Did your parents do this?"

"Look, Karen, I've got to go."

"No." Karen stood, pressed her hands to the glass. "Please, no!"

Ellen sighed. "Just admit that you killed those men," she said. "It's best for everyone."

"I did it for you."

Ellen shook her head. "I've got to go. I brought this for you." She took a package wrapped in brown paper, and gave it to the guard. "Good luck, Karen," she said. She took her phone and hung it up. Karen cried out, but Ellen had turned away, and was motioning to the guard. She did not look back. Karen screamed, and the guards came for her, peeled her off the glass, put her back in a cell. It was over for Karen then, except for a few letters to Ellen that went unanswered. Karen started waiting to die.

The package from Ellen was a book called *One Hundred Years of Solitude*. Karen tried to read the book and understand why Ellen had given it to her, but could not. It was a long story about people far away. But Karen loved the beautiful paper cover. Alone in her cell, Karen traced the tree on the book, the hundreds of leaves, the boat hidden behind the leaves, the glorious angel, the birds, and the snake. The paper was brittle, and worn around the edges.

The trial was a media frenzy, and went on and on. Women crying, saying: *I was waiting for him all night and he never came home...and his wedding ring, oh his wedding ring was gone!...he had said we'd get married someday...my brother was the kindest man, loved dogs and animals...I told him not to take the job! I said, those highways are dangerous at night...*

How did they deal with the fact that their men had pulled over for a quickie? These kind men, these animal-loving men, who cut Karen and hit her and fucked her up the ass. Karen sat still as a statue. Rick pointed at her: *Abused! Childhood trauma! Rape! Battery! Self-defense!* Karen had become a string of exclamations. At night, the voices in the prison rang around her like gunshots.

Karen did not see the papers, but she saw the TV. They called her the "Highway Honey," showing old pictures of her shooting pool, posing for the camera. There was one home video Ellen had made, where Karen lifted her shirt and then laughed, her mouth open. They showed this video a hundred times, blocking out her nipples with a black line. They would slow down her laughter, her open mouth. They made her love menacing and mean. Karen lay awake at night wondering how the reporter had gotten Ellen's video. Could Ellen have given it away?

Rick fought. He was obsessed, his unruly hair, mismatched clothes. And when the jury announced its verdict—it was a skinny blonde with freckles, standing up straight in a blue dress—Rick was the one who crumpled, *guilty, guilty, guilty* ringing in his ears, while Karen remained still. He had expected better, and she had not.

The beautiful woman, Celia Mills, was there the last day, the one whose husband Karen had watched die. Karen had seen her on television: her brown eyes and honey-colored hair. The reporters had a picture of the woman with her husband, somewhere on a beach. The couple was tanned, and the man, the Elvis man, was holding up a fish. The beautiful woman was laughing and clapping her hands.

Celia Mills refused to take the stand, would not speak to reporters. But she had come to the courtroom that last day, and as they sentenced Karen to death, Celia Mills had gazed at Karen steadily. It was the same look her husband had fixed Karen with as he had died. A look of confusion, of disbelief.

Rick came to see Karen periodically, this appeal, that chance, blah, blah, blah. Life went on outside the prison walls, and Rick tried to bring Karen pieces: a bottle of perfume, a magazine, peanut brittle.

Karen doesn't usually talk when Rick visits. She sits with the phone pressed to her ear, listening to his stories and nodding. His crazy hair has gone gray at the edges. Karen knows nothing about his life.

When her meeting with Rick is over and she gets back to Death Row, Karen can feel excitement in the air. Jackie and Veronica are sitting on the patio, and Sharleen is in her cell. Karen realizes that Tiffany is missing.

Jackie looks up from a *House and Garden* magazine. "Tiffany's lawyer came," she says. Karen's heart stops. Is Tiffany going to be set free? Suddenly, Karen feels guilty for not believing in Tiffany, for thinking that Tiffany drowned her babies.

"Maybe we'll never see her again," says Veronica. She does not look happy about the prospect.

"She's guilty as fuck." This is Sharleen. She comes out

of her cell and sinks into a chair. Her hair is growing straight up, and jutting out over her ears.

"Don't come near me," says Jackie.

"You know you want to kiss me," says Sharleen, and then she begins to laugh. Jackie picks up her magazine and goes to her cell.

"Is your attitude really necessary?" says Veronica.

"Oh, are you the new Miss Manners? Miss Death Row Manners?" says Sharleen. She laughs. "How you gonna kill your new boyfriend from the inside, Veronica?" she says.

"Shut your mouth," says Veronica.

"At least I admit what I did," says Sharleen. "Not like the rest of you. At least I'm honest. I have dignity."

There was a silence. "I admitted it," says Jackie, quietly. Karen cannot see her face.

"I have come to peace with God," says Veronica, "and you listen good, Sharleen, I don't give a shit about you."

Sharleen smiles. Her eyes are bright. "Join the club," she says, and then she stands and goes back to her cell. Sharleen has received her execution date, Karen knows.

"Dignity," says Veronica, patting her hair. "Some Satan Killer is going to teach *me* about dignity?"

"Yeah," says Jackie. She comes back out to the table. Opens her magazine.

"I have dignity," says Veronica. "And I have it on the inside, where nobody can touch it."

"Yeah," says Jackie. "Me too."

Karen opens her origami book and looks at the animals she can make with the sheets of paper: swans, peacocks, tigers. She tries to make a small hat, pressing the folds with her index finger. The hat comes out crooked, and Karen puts it under her pillow.

When they hear footsteps in the hallway, the rattle of chains, Sharleen begins to laugh. "Guess you gonna see your Tiffany again," she says. And she is right. Tiffany comes in, her cheeks flushed.

"They're going to do the DNA testing," she says, before the guards unlock her ankle cuffs. "My lawyer got permission. The skin under my babies' fingernails. They'll find out whose it was. They'll let me go home." Her speech is rapid, strange. "This is great," she says. "This is so great!"

"I love you, hon," says Dan when he calls the radio show that week. "I heard about the DNA. Bob told me. We're gonna appeal as soon as the results are in. A few more weeks, honey. And I'll make you enchiladas!" Tiffany sits by the radio with her knees hugged to her chest. She does not do any sit-ups, though. And she does not repaint her nails. Karen listens hard that night, and she isn't sure, but she thinks that maybe, just maybe, Tiffany is crying.

franny

In the early morning, Gatestown seemed asleep. The sky was wide and filled with clouds. It hovered, blue and vast, over the yellow land. Franny looked out the window as her cab drove past the huge courthouse and down the town's quiet streets (passing Poke-E-Jo's Cellular and Guns, the Last Chance Saloon, Tippler's Western Wear) and turned left toward the prison complex. The complex spread above the town like a fortress, rows of stucco buildings like concrete cakes with barbed wire trim.

There were patchy, fenced-in yards where pale women hung their fingers in the fence holes and stared. They all wore gray uniforms, and they were numbered. Inside some of the fences were picnic tables and bright plastic jungle gyms. Franny shivered, thinking of the visiting children sliding down the dusty equipment, trying to pretend they weren't surrounded by barbed wire and fences humming with electricity. In all the years she had lived in Gatestown, she had never been inside the prison.

Mountain View Unit was at the very outskirts of the complex, surrounded by towers in which guards kept watch, their guns trained on the women, ready.

At the gates to the prison, a startlingly young guard asked the cabbie to roll down Franny's window, and then he checked her identification suspiciously. He was younger than Franny, and did not look familiar. He spoke into a walkie-talkie, and then told her to get out of the cab. Franny paid the driver.

A tall man with pale eyes appeared from one of the prison doors and walked briskly to Franny. His blond hair was sculpted into a swooping ducktail hairdo and his pants were just short enough to expose the pale skin above his black socks.

"Miss Wren?" The man's voice was louder than necessary.

"Yes." She shut the cab door behind her, and it began to drive away.

"I'm Guy Hamm, Sergeant of Correctional Officers. Welcome to Mountain View Unit. We're all gonna miss Doc Wren." Hamm's hand was moist. He smelled like pancake syrup.

"Thank you." Franny cleared her throat. "As I said when I called, um, I'm just here to get my uncle's things."

"Not much here besides the car."

Franny nodded.

"I don't need to come in then," Franny said. "If you could just take me to the car. I have the key."

"Some people here would really like to talk to you," said Hamm. He waited, and finally Franny shrugged her acquiescence.

She could not believe how many doors and gates stood

between the inside of the prison and the outside. Hamm wrote their names in three different log books, checking for the exact time on his watch for each book. He unlocked metal doors, waved Franny through, and locked the doors again behind them. Armed guards stood at every turn. The prison smelled of disinfectant, urine, and hot dogs. "Corn dogs for lunch," Hamm told her, pointing into the cafeteria. "But they take the sticks out," he noted.

As Franny and Hamm walked through the prison, Hamm gave a barking commentary: *showers, work room, inmates, watch your back.* It seemed as if the sliding bars never ended. The guards were baby-faced, so young. Franny shook her head. Surely there were people her age who were now guards. Or inmates. But she did not recognize anyone. She felt a familiar guilt: *What if I had spent my life here? What would I have become?*

There were twelve hundred women in Mountain View Unit. Many yelled out when Franny walked past them. The noise was deafening. The women worked in steel cages, chained to chairs, pulling at piles of cotton. They showered in large rooms with drains in the center. They had scorched yards for exercise. Paths had been worn into the dirt around the edges of the fields. "They run in circles," said Hamm, when they passed a window.

The women's cells were small and crowded. Some cells held four women: one slept on each cot and one slept on the floor underneath each cot, with a few inches to breathe. When Franny paused outside a cell where a very pregnant woman sobbed with her head in her hands, Hamm pulled

Franny away. "Medical Center's this way," he said. "Want a soda?"

"No, thank you," said Franny. She could not imagine Uncle Jack in this place.

The Medical Center was clean and neat. Three nurses stood in a circle around a white desk. One had her elbows on the desk, listening to an animated story another was telling, her eyebrows lifted, her mouth ready to smile. When Hamm brought Franny into the room, the nurses stood up straight, looking guilty. Franny recognized one of them as Deborah, the red-haired woman from the hospital. Deborah came toward Franny, and Hamm picked up the phone on the desk. "Warden?" he said into the receiver. "She's here."

"How are you?" said Deborah. "I guess that's a stupid question," she said.

"Look," said Franny, "I'm just here to get my uncle's things. If you could tell me where his car is, I'll be on my way."

Deborah's face closed as if she'd been slapped.

"The warden wants to have a word," said one of the other nurses.

Franny sighed and sat down on a folding chair. She heard footsteps, and looked up to see two guards coming into the Medical Center, holding a woman by the upper arms. The woman's face was ashen. She was extremely thin, and where her head came out of her jumpsuit, Franny could see her collarbones in stark relief. "She's sick again," said one of the guards.

"Jesus," said a nurse. The woman looked at the floor, as if she were ashamed.

"Put her on a cot in the back," said the nurse. "I don't know what else we can do."

Franny folded her arms over her chest, and watched as the guards dragged the woman to a back room, where they let her lie down, still shackled. "She's HIV-positive?" said Franny. The nurse nodded. "Do they have meds for them here?"

"We have them," said the nurse, "but it's hard to know who to give them to. The inmates don't get tested regularly."

"She needs them, obviously," said Franny, gesturing to the woman on the cot.

"She's on Death Row," said the nurse. She added quickly, "But I'm sure she gets the medication she needs."

"Want a soda?" said Hamm, again. Franny did not answer.

Franny had never thought of herself as sexist, but when the slender black woman in a blue uniform walked into the Medical Center it did not even occur to Franny that the woman could be the warden until she introduced herself. She walked straight to Franny, offering her a warm smile and a strong handshake. "I'm Warden Janice Gaddon," she said.

"Franny Wren."

"Dr. Wren, I can't tell you how heartbroken we are about your uncle. I hope you know how much we relied on him." Warden Gaddon shook her head sadly. "I can't quite believe it," she said.

"Well," said Franny, "I'm just here to get the car."

"Do you have a few minutes?"

"I suppose so."

"My office is this way." As she led Franny down the

hallway, the warden left waves of silence in her wake. The inmates glanced down or said hello, quietly. Warden Gaddon looked straight at them and nodded a crisp reply. Her boots made a steady sound as she walked. Next to her, Franny felt young and weak.

The warden signed another log book before walking through a gate, and then they reached a steel door. "Here it is," said Warden Gaddon. She fit a key into the door and opened it. Cold air spilled over Franny. She realized for the first time that the rest of the prison was not air-conditioned.

In marked contrast to the concrete walls and metal bars, Warden Gaddon's office was carpeted and homey. There were framed pictures of children on the wall, and law books shared space with cooking magazines on the bookshelf. There was a coffee maker and a bowl of mints.

"Coffee?" Franny nodded, and Warden Gaddon filled a cup. She sat down behind her desk, gesturing to the couch opposite. Franny sat.

"How long do you think you'll be in Gatestown?" said the warden.

"I have no idea," said Franny. "I really don't know."

"Please let me know if you need anything, will you?"

"Thanks."

"I can't tell you how much I'll miss Jack," said Warden Gaddon, leaning back in her chair. "He was the only one who would come to work in a place like this. Most doctors..." She smiled wryly. "Most reputable doctors, anyway, wouldn't touch this place with a ten-foot pole. Your uncle was a man who spent his whole life in Gatestown, and wanted to give back to the community. He told me so himself." The warden's gaze went to the window, and the field beyond it. Even here, there was no mountain view. "It was at a library fundraiser," said the warden. "Your uncle bought me a beer and we talked for a while. I was new here, and having a tough time of it."

"Where are you from?"

"I'm from Texas, but I never meant to end up as a warden, I can tell you that."

Franny nodded.

"Women's prisons are different. Frankly, I like the men's better."

"Why?"

"There's something catty about the women. I don't know. With the men, it's very straightforward, but with the women there's the...I guess you might say the cunning. Most women prisoners make me nervous." Franny was intrigued. The warden continued, "The first time I had to supervise the showers here, something happened to me. I had supervised hundreds of showers, of course, but not at a women's prison. Men's bodies, it just never bothered me. The first time I saw the women, though, all naked in a row, it made me think of Auschwitz. It was chilling." She paused, and then said, "My God, I'm sorry. We don't even really know each other."

"No, I'm interested. How did you end up here?"

"It's a long story," said the warden, but she did not continue. "Dr. Wren, I don't know what we're going to do without Jack."

"I know," said Franny. There was a silence, and then the phone rang and the warden answered it. Her tone was markedly different: cold, stern. She looked at Franny and rolled her eyes. "No," she said. "You tell him the rule is long pants and I don't care if he has to go to Wal-Mart in Waco. What? All right, I'm coming." She hung up the phone. "Problems at the front gate," she said, standing. "Can I walk you out?" Franny stood.

"Here's my home phone," said the warden, scribbling a number on the back of her card and handing it to Franny. "And call me Janice, please." The warm voice was back, and Franny nodded.

After Janice had escorted Franny back out through the astonishing number of gates and bars and to Uncle Jack's Cadillac, Franny started the car and began to drive. Uncle Jack's house was only a few miles from the prison, but she did not turn, drove right past the Motor Inn, past the Last Chance Saloon. The houses were mostly small and one-level. The car radio scanned from one country station to another. Flushed men and women watered their lawns and walked dogs. Everyone was sweating. Franny tried to recognize people, but no one looked familiar. It felt good to be driving. The air coming in the window smelled of grass.

On the corner of Farm Road 116 and Oak Street, a blue building caught Franny's eye: Gatestown Public Library. She pulled into a parking spot. The library was open, and Franny felt a small thrill. She and Uncle Jack had come to the library a hundred times.

Franny pulled open the screen door, and then the wooden one. She peeked in. To her left, on mismatched recliners, two elderly men in Stetsons sat reading the paper. One looked up, "Come on in, honey," he said. "They're open." Franny blushed and stepped inside.

To her right, rows of colorful books lined the shelves. The sign above them said MYSTERIES. An elderly woman with white hair filed cards at a tall desk. Behind her, more shelves stretched into another room. The woman said, "Welcome to the Gatestown Public Library, dear."

"Hi," said Franny. "Thanks." She pretended to look at the mysteries.

"You here for the Satan Killer?" asked one of the men.

"No," said Franny.

"Here for the Hairdresser of Death?"

"No," said Franny. She looked more intently at the row of mysteries, finally choosing one called *Murder in Manhattan.*

"That's a good one," said the librarian. "My name's Louise."

Franny smiled. "I'm Franny," she said, "Franny Wren." Louise's hand was warm and soft.

"You related to Doc Wren?" said one of the men.

Franny nodded. "I'm his niece."

"I'll be goddamned," said the man. His face was lined and brown. "Little Franny Wren! You used to come into my pharmacy and buy lipstick."

Franny smiled. "Yup," she said. "That's me."

"My son—he was near your age, Donny? He took over

the pharmacy and sold it to CVS. He and that wife of his."

"Well," said Franny.

"How is the Doc?" said the man.

"Oh," said the elderly librarian, covering her mouth with her hand.

"What?"

"He's dead," said Franny. She blinked. "Do I need a library card?" she said. Her voice was unsteady.

Louise waved her hand, a dismissal. "Just bring it back," she said.

Franny nodded, and then saw a book on the shelving cart: *Our Death Row Women*. "What's that?" she said, pointing.

"Oh," said Louise, "I put that together myself." She pulled out the book. It was a collection of newspaper clippings about the women on Death Row, photocopied and bound.

"May I borrow it?"

Louise smiled. "Well, sure," she said. "But I've got to add in the Satan Killer. So bring it back real soon."

"I will," said Franny.

"Hey," said the brown-faced man. "I really am sorry. Your uncle was a good man. He was a fine man to this town."

"I know," said Franny.

By the time Franny got back to Uncle Jack's house it was noon. She slowed to turn into the driveway, but then stopped. There was a rental car parked outside the house with a man inside it: Nat. Franny hit the gas and drove straight to the Gatestown Motor Inn. Her mind whirled; she needed to get her thoughts in order before talking to Nat.

The old woman Franny had spoken with the night before was still at the front desk, still knitting. "Need a room, dear?" she said, looking up.

"Yes," said Franny, sliding her credit card across the counter.

"I recommend Andy's Home Cookin' for lunch," said the woman. "They have a delicious meatloaf."

"Thanks," said Franny. The woman had hair like a Dairy Queen vanilla swirl, and looked to be knitting a large hat.

"I'm just learning," she said, holding up the yarn. Franny nodded, and the woman handed her a room key. "You here for the Hairdresser of Death?" she asked.

"No," said Franny, suddenly very tired. "I am not here for the Hairdresser of Death."

"Don't get upset, dear. I'm Betty. Welcome to Gatestown." She held out a tiny hand. Franny took it.

In Room 17, Franny found a double bed, a plastic desk with a yellow chair, a chest of drawers, and a hot plate. In the bathroom, there was a clawfoot tub. There was no shower. The toilet seat had a fuzzy orange cover.

Franny looked out the window of the motel room. She could see Andy's Home Cookin', a flat building with a giant metal bull rising on a pole from its roof; the Last Chance Saloon, and Woolworth's. Once in a while, someone came out of the saloon, but otherwise, there was a deathly quiet. After a time, she lay down on the bed.

Franny dreamed of her parents. In the dream, the three

of them were in a canoe on the Guadalupe River, with a cooler of chicken salad sandwiches and iced tea. Franny's mother read to her from *Pinocchio*, and her father fished with bait that smelled like the worst thing in the world. It was very hot, but Franny's father kept covering her with blankets. The blankets were itchy and smelled like mothballs. Even though Franny was boiling, she could not take off the blankets. She was immobile. Franny's mother wore her hair in pigtails, and her father wore a straw hat. His hands were red, and large. He kept reaching for Franny. "I'm hot," said Franny in the dream, "It's so hot," but her mother only shook her head. Finally, her mother jumped out of the canoe and into the clear river. Franny was left alone with her father and hot, hot, hot.

celia

Oh, Maureen would have a field day with this. I don't even know what she would come up with: Freudian impulses? The need to protect a child? Some desire to protect myself? I'm sure there's a long and convoluted explanation for why I found myself having sex with a wannabe novelist boy on his ratty futon, but I have only one word to describe it: lust.

Yes, lust! I'm not afraid to say it. I hadn't had sex since Henry, and this boy knew what he was doing. (I did check his driver's license—twenty—not old enough to buy beer but old enough that I wasn't doing anything illegal.) I knew, even upon waking up in the middle of the afternoon in a student apartment on West Campus, that I'd probably read about myself, the next Mrs. Robinson, widow seducer, in the *New York Times Book Review.* But the strange thing is that I do not care. What do I have to lose, really? Well, my job, okay, but when I tallied up a fabulous tryst versus my dull job, I willingly followed the boy home.

The best part about having sex with the novelist-to-be was that, when I sat up in his futon, pulling his cheap red sheets around me, I actually felt as if I were young again. I felt as if I could smoke a joint and read a bunch of Milton and write an incoherent paper and have nothing more to worry about. As if I could head back to the coffee shop where I had drank so many lattés that my stomach had begun cramping and my heart had begun to hammer in my chest, and this boy and I could discuss Proust and dreams and suburbs versus urban living and how many kids, etc. Maybe it was the orgasm, or the smell of dirty laundry that permeated the boy's apartment. Whatever it was, I loved it.

(The boy's name is Marc, with a "c." He's from Amarillo, and—surprise—wants to be the next Paul Bowles or Graham Greene, he hasn't decided yet. Or maybe the next Hemingway, but he isn't sexist, he insisted. Oh, this new generation of enlightened men!)

I climbed from Marc's futon and found my clothes on the floor. In the bathroom (Marc used expensive shampoos and, to my dismay, had a little blue hairdryer, but hairdos like his do not come easily) I gargled with Scope and used the Visine that was next to it on the sink. I opened the medicine cabinet, just out of curiosity, like everyone does, although they will insist that they do not.

Marc had lip balm, sunscreen, shaving gel, a bottle of cologne called Kubla Khan, Advil, NyQuil, and Ritalin, the drug for kids with no attention span. Well, how was Marc going to be a novelist if he had no attention span? And wasn't Ritalin supposed to take away sex drive? (I read this in *Time* magazine, as well.) Maybe Marc had a roommate—who knew?

As soon as I was clothed, I felt old again, and also a bit ridiculous. Marc was still asleep, his mouth open but silent. I tiptoed to the door (it's been a long time since I have tiptoed, and I enjoyed it) and left.

It was not until I was in my car driving back home that I remembered: I had left my letter to Karen Lowens on my boy-toy's bedroom floor.

karen

Evening in Mountain View Unit: the light no different from day. The cell doors are open, and Veronica and Tiffany are sitting on the patio, listening to the radio. Sharleen grunts as she does push-ups in her cell, but nobody is brave enough to tell her to be quiet. Karen sits inside her cell, trying to ignore the waves of nausea and pain. A doctor came from Waco for the day, but did not have time to see Karen.

"Hi, Gerald?" says a lady on the radio show.

"Yes, hello?" says Gerald.

"Um, I just wanted to send some wishes to that lady on Death Row." Tiffany looks up from painting her nails, and Veronica raises her eyebrows.

"Go right ahead, ma'am."

"That lady, the one who killed her husband and kids?" Tiffany goes back to her magazine. Jackie appears at the door to her cell, smiling. Her red hair is wet from the shower.

"Yes?" says Gerald.

"Um, she's getting executed in a week. I guess I just wanted to tell her I'm sorry for her."

"Do you know her, ma'am?"

"No, I'm just sad for her."

"Jackie," calls Veronica, "you got a phone call, honey!" Jackie comes to sit by Veronica, and Tiffany offers to paint her nails. Jackie holds out her stubby hand.

"You're getting so nice, honey," says Veronica, "now that you're about to die." Jackie shrugs. It is true. Jackie has stopped antagonizing everyone, and has even sat through Veronica's fake stories about why all her husbands died so suddenly. Everyone feels strange, now that Jackie's execution date is nearing.

Tiffany's husband has already called the radio show, of course, with more promises of fabulous dinners for Tiffany's return home. Tiffany listens with a half-smile.

Most of the radio show callers are for men: wives and girlfriends, occasionally a heartbreaking mother. One woman promises she'll run right over to the ATM and get bail money for her boyfriend.

"What's an ATM?" says Veronica.

"I have no idea," says Jackie.

"The world is getting complicated," says Veronica. "Like the Internet thing. The Web. What is that all about?"

"You fuckers are pathetic," says Sharleen, in the midst of a round of squats.

"Sor-ry!" says Jackie.

"It's about, like, communication," says Tiffany. "Dan made me a Web page."

"I got a Web page," says Jackie.

"What's a Web page?" says Veronica.

"Who cares?" says Sharleen.

Gerald announces that he has a call for Veronica.

"Hey!" says Jackie.

"The women are winning tonight," says Gerald. "Caller, go ahead."

"Um, Veronica?" It's Jimmy Quinton.

"Hi, honey," says Veronica, touching her neck.

"I don't know if you, um, remember," says Jimmy, "but this is our six-month anniversary." Veronica smiles, and Tiffany winks, impressed.

"Well, Veronica, you're the most..." He stops, clears his throat.

"Most what, honey?" says Veronica. She pats her hair. She really looks more like a kindly grandmother than a killer, thinks Karen.

"I just, I love you, Ronnie. And I know that you love me." Veronica nods. Her eyes are closed, and her smile spreads like butter over her droopy skin.

"So," says Jimmy, "well, Ronnie, I wanted to ask you, um, to be my wife. Will you marry me?"

Veronica's eyes snap open. "Oh my Gooood!" screams Tiffany, jumping up to hug Veronica.

Karen can't help it. She catches Jackie's gaze, and they

both begin to laugh. Why would someone marry Veronica? It's crazy, and yet here is Jimmy Quinton, vying to be husband number eight.

"What are you going to say?" Tiffany's voice is squealing, grating.

"Oh, honey," says Veronica, "I never could say no."

franny

There was a moment, when Franny woke from her nap, in the Gatestown Motor Inn, that she forgot where she was. She felt light, and then she remembered that Anna was dead, that her relationship with Nat was falling apart, and that Uncle Jack was gone. The knowledge came down on her like a rock. And Nat was parked in front of Uncle Jack's house.

On the way to the house, she stopped at the Spurs Gas Mart, and found a bottle of Gallo white wine. The clerk was wearing a baseball hat that said SKOAL. He looked at Franny's bottle.

"You got some ID?" he said.

"Um, OK," said Franny. She took out her wallet, unfolded it, and pushed it across the counter.

"New York?" said the cashier. He made a sound that sounded like "huh."

"Yes, New York," said Franny. "But I'm really from here."

The cashier snorted, and slid the wine into a plastic bag. "Sure, ma'am," he said.

◆ ◆ ◆

Nat's rental car was still at the house, and inside it, he was asleep. Franny knocked on the window and Nat's head jerked up. His hair was matted, and his eyes were rimmed with red.

"Hi," said Franny, when he opened the door.

"Hi," said Nat.

"Do you want to come in?"

"Yeah." He climbed from the car, stretching his arms above his head. He smelled of sleep and beer.

"Have you been drinking?" Franny asked.

"Do you blame me?"

At Uncle Jack's kitchen table, they drank wine from water glasses. "I'm so confused," said Nat. "I've been calling and calling. You unplugged the phone."

"I needed to sleep."

"And what about me, Franny? Did you think about me?"

"I don't know what to say, Nat."

"Well, are we putting off the wedding?"

Franny sipped her wine. "I don't belong there, not really. I've asked Jed for a leave of absence."

"What?"

"And you don't belong here. That's what it comes down to, Nat."

"That is complete crap, Fran. We can live wherever you want. You want me to move to Texas? Is that what you want?"

"No," said Franny, too quickly.

"Then what?"

Franny rubbed her eyes with her fingers. "Sometimes I can't take it," she said. "How everything changes so fast."

"Oh, honey," said Nat, leaning toward her and taking her hands in his. Franny felt trapped. Nat's smell was wrong, his voice, she wanted him gone.

He tried to kiss her, and instinctively, she turned away. "What is it, Fran?"

"I'm sorry."

He stood. He looked lost and angry, like a little boy denied a treat. "Are you really saying it's over?"

"Yes."

"This is the last time," he said, his jaw tight.

"I know."

"Goodbye, Franny," said Nat. He ran his hands through his hair, drained his glass of wine, and walked out. "I'll mail your things," he added, before slamming the door. After a moment, he yanked it open again. "What about your fucking cat?" he said.

"I don't know," said Franny.

"You are one selfish bitch," said Nat. Franny held her breath until she heard the engine start and the wheels backing out of the driveway.

"I'm sorry," said Franny, but all she felt was relieved, numb, and hungry.

She had eaten at Andy's Home Cookin' many times. It would comfort her, she hoped. The metal bull hovering twenty feet above Andy's was larger than life, and "AHC" was painted on its ribcage in a swirling script. The parking lot was filled with trucks. Many of the trucks had dogs waiting in the cabs. As soon as Franny pushed open the door, she was stopped by a teenage girl with her hair in a banana clip. "Welcome to Andy's," the girl said cheerily. "Do you have a reservation?"

"No," said Franny.

"OK," said the girl. She cracked her gum. "You want a booth?"

"Sure," said Franny.

"You're alone?"

"Oh yes," said Franny. "I am alone."

Andy's looked the same as she remembered. On every wall, there were deer heads, and most of them had baseball hats stuck on their antlers. In between the deer heads were sawblades with nature scenes painted on them and large wagon wheels. Also, photographs of men in sunglasses kneeling next to dead deer. In the rare spots where it was visible, the wallpaper was striped.

"Here we go," said the teenager, pointing to a huge table. "No booths free," she said. The table was big enough for fifteen. Franny pulled out a chair and sat. Above her, ten televisions showed reruns of Texas A&M football games. Most tables were filled with chattering families, pitchers of iced tea, plates of chicken-fried steak. Every man had a hat on, either a cowboy hat or a baseball cap. Franny remembered coming to eat here with Uncle Jack and feeling humiliated that her family was so small, just two.

A woman in a tight T-shirt and a jean skirt came to Franny's table. "You waiting?" she said.

"No," said Franny. "It's just me."

"Oh," said the waitress. She was very tan and had plucked most of her eyebrows, leaving only a thin, arching line.

"I'll have a Bud." The woman nodded, and walked away. Franny opened the menu. Meatloaf, ribs, double cheeseburger, ham.

Franny ordered the meatloaf, which was heavy and dry. She ate all of the mashed potatoes with gravy, and the butter beans. She finished her beer, and ate another bite of meatloaf.

At the next table, a man in a Dr. Pepper baseball cap sat next to a tall woman with a red nose. The red-nosed woman elaborated loudly on the merits of Baco-Bits. In her opinion, there were many. Franny decided to go through her wallet. She took out her New York Public Library card and a Blockbuster Video coupon. She ate another bite of meatloaf. The bacon discussion segued into a debate: McDonald's versus Arby's. Franny took the picture of Nat from her wallet and studied it. She felt strangely peaceful.

Where was Franny's waitress? She seemed to have disappeared. The television started playing another football game: the A&M Aggies against Notre Dame. "There's no roast beef at Micky D's!" said the man in the Dr. Pepper hat. "You can have your Ronald McDonald, honey!"

Franny stood, and walked to the front of the restaurant. There, the girl with the banana clip sat behind a cash register. "Seven-fifty," she said to Franny.

"What?"

"Meatloaf, Bud, seven-fifty," said the girl.

Franny pulled out a ten. The sign above the cash register said, "Local Checks Only NO Credit Cards NO Diner's Club."

When she received her change, Franny went back to leave a tip. Her table had been cleared already, its surface wiped clean and shining.

In bed, Franny leafed through *Our Death Row Women* as she waited for sleep to come. Growing up in Gatestown, she had never really thought about the women in the prison. Among her grade school classmates there was an unspoken agreement to ignore the prison's existence. When Uncle Jack had told her he was going to take a few afternoons away from his practice and volunteer at the prison, she had been surprised. "Time to give back, feels like," he had explained.

Our Death Row Women was primarily made up of articles from *People* and the *Gatestown Messenger*. Franny felt as if she were in a movie, looking at the pictures of crazy women who were living just a few blocks away, eating, sleeping, dreaming. She drank wine and leafed through the pages until she came to Karen, who Franny recognized as the woman who had come into the Medical Center while Franny had been waiting for the warden. They called Karen the "Highway Honey." In the picture from *People*, she was skinny, with sad eyes.

The article said that Karen Lowens was a serial killer,

one of the few female serial killers in Texas history. She had grown up in a desperately poor household, and started prostituting when she was twelve. Her first known murder was in 1988, when she was twenty. She worked along the side of the highway, approaching men at rest stops or along the road. She lived with her lover, Ellen Girand, in the Hi-D-Ho Motel in South Austin. Karen supported Ellen, who was a junkie.

There was a picture of Karen and Ellen together, in a bar. Ellen, who was lovely, with long curled hair and blue eyeshadow, was talking to someone, but it was Karen's face that stopped Franny's heart. Karen gazed at Ellen with such awe and yearning. *I've never loved anyone like that,* thought Franny. She felt a sharp pang of jealousy, before she remembered where Karen had ended up.

Karen was due to be executed on August twenty-fifth, less than six weeks away.

Franny turned the page to see a picture of Karen as a young girl. *Karen Lowens, future serial killer, at six years old,* the caption said, *outside her trailer in Uvalde, Texas, 1974.*

1974: It was the same year Franny's parents had died. At age six, in small Texas towns, Franny and Karen had been the same.

On the last page of *Our Death Row Women,* Louise the librarian had compiled a list of names and food. As Franny read down the list she began to feel sick. Written in Louise's neat cursive, it was the last meals ordered by executed male prisoners:

Ed Skooner: 2 chicken-fried steaks with white gravy, french fries, 4 pieces of white bread, apple, 2 Cokes.

Brendan James Young: Double cheeseburger, french fries topped with cheese, baked potato topped with sour cream, cheese, and butter, 2 fried pork chops, 3 beef enchiladas, chocolate cake.

Aaron Lonn: 1/2 pound of chitterlings, fried chicken (dark meat), 10 slices of bacon, 1 raw onion, fried shrimp, peach cobbler, 1 pitcher whole milk.

Kerry Polender: Beef fajitas, stir-fry beef, 6 cinnamon rolls, 1 pecan pie, 1 cherry pie, 1 diet cream soda, 3 eggs.

Steven Morris: Salmon croquettes, scrambled eggs, french fries, biscuits.

Dennis King: Venison steak, baked potato, Lite beer. (Water substituted. Alcohol prohibited by TDCJ policy.)

José Robles: Heaping portion of lettuce, 1 sliced tomato, 1 sliced cucumber, 4 celery stalks, 4 sticks of American or cheddar cheese, 2 bananas, 2 cold half-pints of milk. Asked that all vegetables be washed prior to serving.

Gary B. Waldon: God's saving grace, love, truth, peace, and Freedom.

Martin Hewett: Barbecued chicken, refried beans, brown rice, sweet tea, bubble gum. (No gum. Bubble gum is not permitted under TDCJ regulations.)

Clay Dellacort: Steak, french fries, wine. (Water substituted. Alcohol prohibited by TDCJ policy.)

◆ ◆ ◆

Franny could just see Louise, carefully writing this list. Where had she gotten this information? Why the hell couldn't they allow someone a glass of wine? Franny imagined the man's face, when he saw that water had been substituted.

On her bedside table, Franny had dumped the contents of her pockets. There, amidst loose change and a receipt from lunch, was Warden Gaddon's card, her home phone number written in green pen.

Franny picked up the phone and slowly dialed the number. "Janice?" she said, when the warm voice answered. "Janice, it's Franny Wren."

The next night, Franny drove her uncle's car to Janice Gaddon's house. She idly turned the radio dial, trying to find an appealing song. The air-conditioner hummed, and Franny turned the headlights on. The twin lights brushed over the ground. In the distance, the prison loomed, yards glowing, guard towers lit at the top like candles. The warden had said that her house was farther on down the same road as the prison. Franny did not see any women in the yards.

The warden's house was one-story, and her car, a red Taurus, was parked in the driveway. Franny parked behind it, and stepped out of the Cadillac. The night air smelled of approaching rain.

In Janice's yard was a large, low oak tree with a porch swing hung from its branches. The house was built of pale limestone. Franny walked up the path of narrow stones. The door was wooden, and painted gray. There was a brass mail slot in the center. Franny knocked.

"Hi," said Janice, opening the door, and letting the smell of tomato sauce escape into the damp evening. "Come in," she said. Janice wore her hair down over a gray cable-knit sweater. With jeans and bare feet, she looked years younger than she had in the prison. She was holding a wine glass.

"Can I pour you some?" she asked, and Franny nodded. The entrance hall to Janice's house was painted yellow and had hardwood floors. "Come on into the kitchen," said Janice.

Franny followed her, past a framed Jasper Johns poster and pictures of a teenage boy with curly hair. "That's my son, Daven," said Janice, stepping over a baby gate that was stretched across the kitchen entrance. Franny followed, and was immediately jumped on by a giant dog.

"For God's sake!" said Janice. "Sorry about him. Harrison, sit!" She looked apologetically at Franny.

"What is he?" said Franny, accepting a glass of white wine and looking around the large kitchen.

"A Burnese Mountain Dog," said Janice. "Stuck in Texas," she added. She patted the dog roughly, and then moved to the stove, where a large pot bubbled. Janice lifted the lid.

"Smells wonderful," said Franny. The wine was cold in her mouth.

Janice laughed. "It's from a jar," she said, pointing to the empty Ragu bottle on the counter. "I can't cook a damn thing," she said. "One of the many reasons my marriage ended." Her smile was rueful.

"What a nice kitchen," said Franny. The floor and walls were tiled in blue and white.

"Thanks," said Janice. "The wife of the last warden was big on dinner parties. She got the tiles in Mexico."

"How long have you been here?"

"Four years. I was in Huntsville before—one of the first female guards."

"Really?"

Janice stirred the sauce. "Used to be," she said, "that women couldn't work in men's prisons. My husband was a guard, and the only work I could get was filing papers." She shook her head. "And sewing the sheet," she said.

"The sheet?"

Janice faced Franny. She took a sip of her wine. "When the first man was given lethal injection in Huntsville," she said, "they had some dirty old sheet on the gurney. The warden got all sorts of flack for it when the newspapers published the pictures." She put her hands on her hips. "My husband—John—and I were at a barbecue at the warden's. We had a few beers and got to talking, and the warden asks me if I'll sew a new sheet for the gurney. Can you believe it? But what could I do? We needed money, so I sewed the sheet. Cut out all the holes—for the straps, you know—with my pinking shears."

Franny did not know what to say. "I know, not like life in New York, is it?" Janice said. Franny shrugged. She suddenly felt that calling Janice had been a terrible idea. She wished she could leave, go back to her uncle's house, pack her bags, and head somewhere else. Or at least go back to her uncle's house and get drunk.

"I'm so glad you called," said Janice.

"Yes, well," said Franny.

"When are you going back to New York?"

"I don't know," said Franny. Her eyes filled with tears, and she blinked them back. Janice came close to Franny, and folded her in her arms. Franny flinched, but then gave in to Janice's warmth. Janice smelled of garlic and shampoo. "I miss him," said Franny, her face pressed into Janice's collarbone. "I don't think I knew him, in the end."

"Shhh," said Janice.

"It's true," said Franny, wiping beneath her eyes. "I left here so long ago, and I never came home, or asked about his life."

"He loved you very much. He talked about you," said Janice.

"Really?"

"Oh, honey," said Janice. "You were his whole world." She took Franny's glass and refilled it. "Why don't you just relax," she said. "Just sit at the table there and read some catalogs. Then we'll have spaghetti. What do you say?"

Franny nodded. She sat down and opened a Lillian Vernon catalog. Janice's kitchen was warm.

After they had eaten, they went into Janice's backyard, so Janice could have a cigarette. She offered Franny one and Franny took it. They sat on lawn chairs, listening to crickets.

"Are you happy in New York?" asked Janice.

Franny thought for a moment. "I don't know," she said finally. Franny looked at Janice, her kind eyes. "How did you end up here?" she said.

Janice paused, as if deciding something. "I married John when I was eighteen," she said, "I was pregnant, and I thought I loved him. I grew up in a tiny town west of here. Lovelady." She took the bottle of wine they had brought outside with them, refilled her glass and then Franny's, settling the bottle between her feet on the ground. She leaned her head back. "Look at the stars," she said. Franny looked up, saw the bowl of sky dusted with silver.

"I went away to school," said Franny, "when I was sixteen."

Janice nodded, sipped her wine. When Franny did not continue, Janice said, "Well, my marriage was fine, at first. John got the job in Huntsville, and I was happy at home, for a while. But the prison changes you."

"Changes you?" said Franny. "What do you mean?"

"You spend all day enforcing rules. Especially in the men's prisons, it can get violent. You can smell the aggression—it's everywhere, this potential for a fight. To keep order, you end up treating the inmates like children. When they disobey, you punish them, usually with force." Franny was silent, and Janice went on. "John didn't start out as a violent man. I believe that. But he had it in him, and eventually, he began to bring it home."

"He hit you?"

"It was what he knew. When the baby acted up, he

didn't know how to reason anymore. He told me it was the same as the inmates, that he couldn't handle messiness anymore, in any part of his life. The lines began to blur in his mind. Of course he was always sorry."

"So you left him," said Franny.

"I wish I could tell you that, but it isn't true. John left me, and the baby, fell for someone else. I was so young, we both were. So I got a job, and eventually they let women become guards, and then…"

"Warden."

"I'm one of the only female wardens in the state," said Janice.

Franny felt lightheaded. "Do you…take it home?" she asked.

"Not yet," said Janice. "Maybe some people have it in them and some don't."

Franny was silent. "How often did my Uncle Jack come to the prison?" she asked finally.

"Once a week. We're desperate without him. Most of the doctors who apply to work in prisons…" She shook her head. "Your uncle was one of a kind. He really cared about the women, raised their standard of care. But now, I don't know what will happen."

Franny took a long sip of her wine. She opened her mouth, but then closed it.

"What?" said Janice.

Franny shook her head. "Nothing."

Janice turned to Franny, put a hand on her hand. "Please," said Janice. "What?"

There was a quiet moment, and then Franny said, "I could come in. I could help. Just until you find a permanent replacement. Why not?"

"Are you serious?"

"I don't know," said Franny. And then she said, "Yes."

celia

I was talking to Henry's parents and eating a peach. "I just don't think it's necessary," I told them. They were calling from their home in Vermont. I was resting my feet on Priscilla, who was on the floor. Priscilla did not like summer. She lay on her back, exposing her pink stomach and wriggling around. The whole street smelled sweet, and azaleas burst like fireworks from their buds. It was almost shameful in Texas this time of year. Everything open, lusty, and raw.

"We need to see it," said Henry's mother, Ursula. "I'm not proud of it, Celia, but there it is." I sighed, and looked at Henry's watering can. I could not remember the last time I had touched it. Henry's gardening tools still hung in a row in the garage. I hired a neighbor boy named Seth to mow the lawn every other week, but let the garden go to hell. I couldn't bear to kneel down in that fertile soil, the smell reminding me. Henry's tomato vines were wild; I asked Seth to leave those alone.

"We're looking at plane fares," added Henry's father.

"Can you recommend a place to stay there in…" Ursula paused.

"Huntsville," I said. "They take them to Huntsville."

"Yes," said Ursula. "Huntsville, Texas. Where do we even fly in?"

Henry's parents had never come to visit us during our marriage. They had been angry about the elopement, horrified to hear about Vegas and the Elvis chapel. I hadn't met them in person until their son was already dead. "I'll do some planning," I said. "Why don't you fly in here? I can show you around…"

"Celia!" cried Ursula. "This is hardly a sightseeing tour."

"Oh, right," I said.

"Jesus," said Henry's father. "What's the matter with you?" I knew they saw me as some hussy Henry had fallen for. I knew they thought his short time with me meant nothing, and the Henry they knew was all the Henry there was.

My mother felt the same way about me, asked me often when was I coming home to Wisconsin, where I belonged. But I have changed, and I belong in Texas now, where I knew Henry. Where I loved him, and where we sat on our porch swing and watched the moon.

"Well," I said. "Keep me posted, will you?"

"Yes, dear," said Ursula. She was a hippie who still wore her hair long and parted in the middle. She made batik T-shirts to sell at craft fairs despite the fact that she was rich. She drove a VW van, and only used the Miata when the VW broke down.

"I'm sorry to snap at you," said Ursula. "I'm just edgy. It's not your fault."

"You think it *is* my fault, though, don't you?" I said. I bit my lip, and looked at Priscilla, who stood and raised her eyebrows at my audacity. I sipped my Coke and listened to the flustered silence.

"What?" said Henry's father.

"Did we hear you correctly?" said Ursula.

"Forget it," I said. Priscilla sighed and sank down, all four paws stretched against the floorboards.

I saw a figure come walking up the street with a loping gait. I recognized with a mixture of horror and happiness that it was my boy, Marc. (Does he mow lawns, I wondered? For a split second, I imagined keeping him around, letting him write all day while I brought him martinis and typed his manuscripts on one of those old typewriters that clicks away romantically. I would be the Sugar Momma with my big librarian salary.)

"I'm going to have to run," I said into the phone. Ursula sniffed. "So, keep me posted," I said.

"August twenty-fifth, then?" said Henry's father. "Do you think she'd ask for an appeal at the last minute?"

"Some of them do that, you know," said Ursula.

"I have no idea," I said. "How could I have any idea?"

"Goodbye, dear," said Ursula, and I heard her phone line click. I knew that Henry's father was in for a big rant.

"Goodbye," I said. Henry's father hung up without saying anything. A month after the wedding, he had asked me to call him "Dad."

◆ ◆ ◆

I swung on my porch swing, bit into my peach. Marc waved shyly and ambled up the walk. Priscilla lifted her head, gave me that tilted look of curiosity, and then watched Marc. Perhaps she thought he was selling candy bars for Little League. Perhaps she thought he had come to check the termite stations, or deliver a package. Perhaps Priscilla even knew that Marc and I were summer lovers. The song "Summer Loving" from *Grease* popped into my head. I bit down laughter and noted that I was heading rapidly toward certifiable. This was turning into some weekend, all right. And then he was standing before me, his pretentious hairdo as cute as ever.

He held my letter to Karen Lowens in his hand. "Your address," he said sheepishly.

"Thanks," I said.

"Nice house," he said. I nodded. He said, "Nice dog." He smelled of all his lotions and cologne. Henry had never even worn deodorant. The boy shuffled his feet on my welcome mat.

"Do you want to come in?"

"Yes," said the boy, Marc.

I stood, opened the door. He came inside.

karen

Reporters, reporters, reporters. All of a sudden, everybody cares about Jackie. Karen can't hear the people outside, but she can see them on TV. Helicopters, people with signs, reporters with blond hair and gray comb-overs. Everybody is talking to everybody, and there is Jackie, and she is the same. She is sewing her sequins and staying away from Sharleen. Sharleen has crazy things in her cell: stars drawn with chalk, letters from her Satan Killer boyfriend, Markus. On TV, Markus is scary-looking, even now that they have shaved off his dreadlocks for his court appearances. The letters from Markus have big sections cut out, or covered over with ink. Who knows what those parts say? Karen does not want to know.

It is Jackie's last day. Some strange friends have visited her over the years, and her poor mother, who is white as chalk, but since she killed her whole family, there haven't been too many care packages. Now Jane Pauley and Stone Phillips are staying at the Gatestown Motor Inn. On TV,

Karen sees Andy's Home Cookin' and the Last Chance Saloon. Reporters line the sidewalks, talking to locals, and there is a segment of "Good Morning, America" inside Katie's Koffee Haus. Jackie had her choice of guests on visiting day.

On television, Jackie is calm and pretty. She watches herself, eating Doritos and sitting on a patio chair. "If only I had some conditioner," she murmurs. During TV interviews, she plays with her hair, and when she reaches up, you can see the metal handcuffs.

The interviews take place inside the green room, where there is no glass wall separating Jackie from the reporters. Nobody knows how the media gets permission to visit in the green room. Dan and Jimmy Quinton would like to know.

The reporters pretend to look sympathetic, but Karen can see they are vultures, picking at the little meat left on Jackie's bones. "Are you frightened?" asks one reporter, cocking her head.

Jackie presses her lips together (Tiffany has lent her some lip gloss). "I was insane at the time that the incident occurred," she says. "I should not be put to death. I am begging the governor for mercy."

"But are you afraid?" The reporter sounds concerned.

"Yes," says Jackie. She blinks and tries to cry. She has been practicing in her cell. She says that if she thinks about her mother she can make herself cry. She blinks and blinks, but no tears come. The reporter nods slowly, and then looks at the camera.

"Our time is up," she says. "And now to you, Fred, with an update on the Texas Tech game."

◆ ◆ ◆

Jackie does not seem to believe that they will kill her. Yes, she has sewn her dress, and given interviews, even cried in some, but she does not really think it will be over, bang, like that.

It seems unthinkable. Karen has been on Death Row for five years. Every hour is like the one before it. Everybody knows what their dates are, and the order in which they are supposed to die: Jackie, Karen, Veronica, Tiffany, Sharleen. But nobody has died yet, so they are all safe. They have grown accustomed to the slow, methodical rhythm of their days. In the morning, if Jackie is taken from them, put in her dress and executed—if Jackie is taken, they will all be taken. And Karen will be next.

Karen opens Ellen's book. She runs her eyes for the hundredth time over the first words: "Many years later, as he faced the firing squad, Colonel Aureliano Buendia was to remember that distant afternoon when his father took him to discover ice."

Ice. Karen loves the word. It is so far away from her hot cell, the smell of sweat, and the reality of Jackie's impending death. Karen closes her eyes, and sees a graceful ice skater in her mind's eye, gliding seamlessly over a frozen mirror. The skater has long hair; it streams behind her as she moves, bending her knees and preparing to jump, preparing to hurl herself forward into the cold air.

The news has come: there will be no stay for Jackie. Tonight, a made-for-TV movie based on her life will air. It is called *Hairdresser of Death*. Drew Barrymore is playing Jackie. In the previews, she looks off-balance in a red wig, and sits at a salon having her nails done by Farrah Fawcett. "What's on your mind?" Farrah Fawcett asks Drew Barrymore in the preview. "You look distracted."

Drew gives Farrah a secretive look. "You don't even want to know, Lou Anne," she says, and Farrah says, "Oh Jackie, I do."

Even Jackie agrees that it is good Farrah is back on her feet, playing lead roles. Jackie says her traitorous friend Lou Anne is actually fat as a house and with thin hair to boot, but oh well. As for Drew Barrymore, Jackie is disappointed. She wants Julia Roberts to play her. Even Jennifer Aniston, with a dye job. But the *E.T.* girl? Jackie looks down at her hands. Fuck, she says, the *E.T.* girl.

They know they will not be allowed to watch *Hairdresser of Death*. As soon as it comes on, the secret control room will switch the channel to PBS.

Tiffany and Veronica sit with Jackie in front of the TV. "The governor," says Tiffany. "He could come down any time, Jackie. All he has to do is say the word."

"He ain't going to say shit, Tiffany."

Tiffany opens her bubblegum lips, but remains silent.

"Maybe I should talk to Moira," says Jackie. Moira is the prison chaplain, a thin woman who wears headbands and white blouses. She runs the daily Bible study in Mountain View Unit, arriving in a nervous flurry and reading aloud in a weak voice. After she reads, she says, "Now would anyone like to share some thoughts?" Usually, no one shares anything but complaints about the food or prison conditions, but Moira listens carefully anyway, nodding encouragingly and sighing where appropriate.

"Whatever you want, honey," says Veronica.

Jackie sighs. She seems to grow smaller by the day. "Hey, Satan Killer," calls Jackie. "What do you have to tell me?"

"Nothing," says Sharleen.

"What does Satan have to say about dying?" Jackie makes a sarcastic face, but her tone is sincere.

Sharleen stands and comes to the edge of her cell. She does push-ups and sit-ups and gets bigger every day. Karen is waiting for the day when Sharleen will pull the bars from the floor. "Satan doesn't have no time for your last-minute shit," she says. And then she turns and goes back inside her cell.

"Jesus," murmurs Tiffany. "I mean "jeepers,'" she amends.

Jackie's eyes fill with tears. In the time Karen has known Jackie—twenty-four hours a day for five years—Karen has never seen her this way. Veronica stands up, pulling her elderly bulk along with her. "You've got no business being such a goddamn bitch, Sharleen!" she says, in a voice that is hard, and unlike her. She makes her way to Sharleen's cell.

"What have you got to say about it?" says Sharleen.

"Jackie's going to die tomorrow, Sharleen, and you're going to die, too. I don't care who you are or what you've done, but everybody deserves some kindness on their last day."

Sharleen does not reply.

"Apologize," says Veronica.

Sharleen spits, "Fuck you." She puts her meaty hands on her hips.

Karen closes her eyes. She does not want a fight, not now. The air is already too heavy and dark. But the words come flying, and the smell of ammonia and vomit is tinged with heat, burned. The sounds of slaps and screaming.

The guards come quickly, and Veronica is taken to the Medical Center. Sharleen says, "I'm fine, I'm fine," but they haul her off to solitary. When *Hairdresser of Death* comes on a few hours later, the guards shut off the TV.

Karen does not believe she can find God by meeting with Moira. God is inside, Karen thinks. He becomes visible when you die, to take your hand and lead you to a better place. And yet the silence of the evening, broken only by the shuffling of cards as Jackie and Tiffany play, feels like a gift from someone.

Karen knows how it will be for Jackie. She has imagined it a hundred times. The guards will wake Jackie up, like any other day of the 3,734 she has spent on Death Row. They will wake her, and put the handcuffs on her, and the cuffs on her ankles too. Then they will open the first door, and she will leave.

They take you to The Walls prison in Huntsville, Texas. Karen thinks they drive you, but they keep it a secret: maybe you fly. Karen has never been on a plane. You will see Gatestown, the town they know only from television. Katie's Koffee Haus, the Last Chance Saloon, Andy's: all the places the guards talk about when they think the women aren't listening: *Let's grab a beer at Last Chance. How about meatloaf at Andy's? Get me some coffee at Katie's!*

Maybe you will see Jane Pauley, standing in the street, getting mud on her pumps. Karen doesn't know. She doesn't know the order of the places, either. She had never been to Gatestown before her sentence, and for all she knows Andy's could be next door to Katie's, or across the street or even on top. There are no windows in Mountain View Unit. Is there a mountain somewhere?

On television, The Walls looks like a frightening place. It is a towering stone structure with a giant clock imbedded above the entrance. Outside The Walls, men who have just been released mingle with reporters and protesters. According to Geraldo Rivera's special report, the Cafe Texan down the street is especially busy on execution days.

Inside The Walls, Jackie will get up to shower and put on her sparkling dress. She will eat her final meal. She deliberated for weeks about what to have, but in the end she chose steak, mashed potatoes, and a glass of champagne. She will not get the champagne.

Karen will ask for only one thing on her last day, a peach. She thinks about it sometimes, the way the ripe flesh will give, spilling juice on her tongue. The first bite of a sweet peach: the closest Karen will come to love.

During the last meal, the death watchers assemble in the lounge. There are the journalists who have won the lottery—the Texas Department of Criminal Justice picks only a few reporters out of the hundreds who apply to witness an execution. There is Marylin Fisket from the *Huntsville Item* who always gets in, and writes pretty nice stuff with no gory details: just the outfit and the last words and the time. If you are a journalist from the town where the murder/rape/etc. was committed, you get first dibs to watch. For example, Jackie's family was killed in Baytown, so Liz Landry from the *Baytown Sun* will get into the execution. (This is OK with Jackie. Liz wrote to Jackie and has done a feature on her once a year, published some of her letters and crummy drawings.) Nobody can record or videotape anything, only memories and pencils allowed.

The condemned (Jackie, in this case) is allowed five witnesses. Jackie will have her mother, a frail lady who looks like a baby bird; her father, a squat man with Jackie's same red hair and Jackie's same meanness; her friends from childhood, Mary and Emily (who wrote letters once in a while and visited infrequently); and a boy named David who wrote Jackie love letters because he is deranged. But Jackie thinks he is cute in the picture he sent (he is leaning against a car and his jeans are tight), so he can watch her die.

Also, the victims' families get to watch. Jackie doesn't talk about her dead husband's parents. Karen guesses they will be there, hoping Jackie's death will bring them something, some kind of peace.

They will give Jackie a tranquilizer first, and Benadryl to stop her from spasms and choking. It is ten paces from the cell to the execution chamber. A tie-down team fastens six leather straps, and an IV team inserts catheters into both forearms. The warden stands at the head of the table, and the chaplain stands at the foot. There is another official whose job is to tell the reporters about your state of mind. "Jackie is calm," he will say, or "The prisoner is agitated."

The needle will go into Jackie's leg. She will have a chance for a final statement, Warden Gaddon will read Jackie's death sentence, and then the Lethal Injection Machine will be turned on, releasing sodium thiopental for sedation, pancuronium bromide to relax Jackie's muscles, and then potassium chloride to stop her heart. The process is four minutes long. When your muscles are asleep, there are still moments that your brain is awake.

"The last breath is the loudest," Karen heard a guard say. "But the eyes," he said, "are the worst. Whatever you do, don't look down into their eyes when they go."

franny

The night before Franny began work at the prison, the parking lot at the Gatestown Motor Inn was full, and she had to park in the street when she went to get a drink. There was a sign taped to the front desk: NO VACANCY.

"What's going on?" asked Franny.

"Execution," said Betty, not even looking up from her knitting.

There were two bartenders on duty in the lounge, and every table was full. Franny scanned the room with awe. Everyone was so good-looking, so well-dressed. Franny thought she recognized a blonde woman from TV, but couldn't place her.

"What a dump, huh?" said a man standing next to Franny in the doorway. He had thick brown hair, combed carefully and sprayed into place. "I'm Christopher," he said, "*News 2*, Houston." His smile was even, his teeth perfect.

"Franny Wren." She held out her hand.

"Who are you with?" said the man, Christopher, as they

settled on barstools. "Are you local? You don't look familiar."

"I'm not with anyone. I'm a doctor."

To Franny's relief, this seemed to satisfy him. She suddenly felt frumpy in her baggy jeans and cotton sweater. "Can I buy you a drink?" asked Christopher. His face looked as if it were made of plastic: shiny, pink, slick.

"Sure. White wine."

Christopher signaled the bartender, the blond boy, who looked at Franny quizzically. He filled a glass with wine. Franny did not meet his eyes.

"So," said Christopher, "what are you doing here?"

Franny thought fast. "Vacation?" she said. The bartender lifted an eyebrow.

Christopher nodded. Luckily, he did not want to talk about Franny. "Well, you know why I'm here," said Christopher. "The Hairdresser of Death." He sipped his martini. "She gets the needle tomorrow," he said. "As I'm sure you know."

"Oh," said Franny.

"Yeah, I've got to cover the protests, her last meal, last words, et cetera," said Christopher. "Interview the victim's family, the hairdresser's mom, blah, blah." He bit into an olive.

"Blah, blah?" said Franny.

"You're not from here," said Christopher, and without waiting for her response, he said, "Let me tell you something. If it weren't a woman getting the needle, I wouldn't even be here. Executions get boring in Texas." He took out a pack of cigarettes and lit one. "Bo-ring," he said, and then he ordered another martini.

The bar was loud and boisterous. Franny could hear laughter, the clink of ice in glasses. There was a festive atmosphere, as if something wonderful were about to happen. "So you believe in the death penalty?" said Franny.

"Oh, Christ," said Christopher. "I don't have an opinion. You've got to stay impartial, that's the thing. I'm here for the story, the tears, blood and guts." He drew in on his cigarette. "I don't give a shit about the death penalty," he said. "If you want to know the truth."

"But doesn't it make you sad?" she said. "Watching someone die?"

"No," said Christopher.

Franny's wine was dull and sour, but she finished it anyway, and ordered another. Christopher told her about Houston, about television, and eventually about his ex-wife. Franny tried to listen, but kept turning her head, following the sound of raucous laughter. She saw Dan Rather in the corner of the room. The piano player belted out Cole Porter. Christopher smelled like peanuts.

"So my wife, my ex-wife, she tells me I have no depth of feeling," said Christopher. "I ask you, what does that mean?"

Franny shrugged, and drank more wine. Christopher put his hand on her knee, and it was warm. She did not move it. He took her hand, traced its lines. "You're quite beautiful," he said. But when he asked her to his room, she said no.

"I have to get up early in the morning," she said.

Christopher gave her his card. "Call me if you're ever in Houston," he said. "And, you know, if she doesn't get an appeal, the Highway Honey will get the needle in a few weeks, so I'll be back."

Back at Uncle Jack's, Franny picked up the phone. She dialed the area code for Manhattan, but then held the receiver in her hand. She could easily abandon her promise to Janice Gaddon, call the hospital back and cancel her leave of absence. It was so tempting to slip back inside her life in New York. But Franny wanted to understand what had moved Uncle Jack. She wanted to know what she was capable of. Franny bit her lip, and hung up the phone.

celia

"Are you going to mail the letter?" asked Marc. We lay in my bed, bands of light from the window crossing our legs. I knew I should feel ashamed, or at least ridiculous, lying entwined with a young boy, but I felt happy. Happiness: a simple emotion (and surely related to sex) but it had been a long time since I had felt it. I had forgotten how joy could run through your veins.

"I don't know," I said.

"What does the letter say?"

"Are you going to put me in your novel?" I said, pulling my hand away.

He smiled. "That's not really fair," he said. "Besides, it's finished. I sent it off yesterday."

"What's it about?"

"It's a mess of a book about my father, mostly. He's pretty much an asshole. I wrote it to try to figure him out, I think. Isn't everyone's first novel about themselves?" He sat up, and pulled a package of cigarettes from his pants.

"You can't smoke in here," I said, my voice panicked. I was about to say, *because Henry hates cigarettes.*

"I'm sorry."

"It's OK," I said. "You want to read it? The letter to Karen?"

"If you want me to." I stood, pulling the sheet around myself, and went to get the letter. When I brought it back to the bedroom, he had pulled on his clothes, and I felt stupid in the sheet, like some toga queen. It was my house and my lover—I should have felt in control of the situation, but I did not. Suddenly, watching this boy open my letter (taking his John Lennon glasses from the bedside table, sliding them over his nose to read), I felt scared. He read slowly, stopping once to look up at me and smile sadly. I was so tired of being pitied.

After a minute, I couldn't watch. I pulled on a pair of shorts and a top and went to sit on the porch swing. Across the street, Mrs. Murphy (who worked at Sears and set out a recycle bin full of Miller Lite cans every Thursday) sat on her front step, throwing birdseed out over her lawn. She waved to me. "How are you, honey?" she called.

"Fine, Mrs. Murphy!" I said.

"You want a beer, honey?" She held up her can as if to encourage me in daytime drinking. She wore a dingy pink bathrobe and a net of some sort over her hair. A neighbor had told me that Mrs. Murphy had at least seventeen cats, but she didn't let any of them outside. Periodically, her screen door got scratched clear through, and Henry had gone over to help her repair it a few times.

"How many cats did you count?" I once asked him.

"Oh God, a million," he'd said, laughing and putting his hand over his eyes. We had collapsed with laughter, feeling invincible, feeling that our happiness was something we were entitled to.

I told Mrs. Murphy I wasn't ready for a beer yet and she shrugged and opened another for herself. I had almost forgotten about Marc when I looked up and saw him standing inside the door, trying to unlatch it to join me outside. I jumped up, and stepped into the house. "Don't want the neighbors to see me?" said Marc, laughing.

"It's just hot," I said.

"Liar."

"Marc," I said. "I think you should go."

"Hey," he said, taking my shoulders in his hands. I shook my head and blinked back tears.

"Please," I said. "Please just go." He stepped back, his palms open as if waiting for something, a present, a promise.

"Can I call you?"

"I don't think so," I said.

He looked bewildered, but turned to go. Before he stepped out the door, he said, "You wrote a beautiful letter, Celia. You should send it."

"I will," I said. "Thanks." And then he left.

I went into my bedroom and took all the sheets off the bed and put them in the washer. I took the cups we had drunk tea from and washed them clean. There was a message on my answering machine: *Hi, Celia? It's Jenny. I, well, I guess I was hoping you'd come to the baby shower. But, well, maybe we could have lunch? You know the number, anyway. I'll be here.* I pressed the Delete button, erasing the message.

Marc had left my letter on the table by the door. I put it in a new envelope, addressed it, and put it on my desk. I would take the letter to Claudel on Monday, and he would mail it to Death Row.

part three
august

karen

Karen wakes to the sound of metal snapping shut. It is August first, and Jackie is standing outside Karen's cell. The guards hold Jackie tightly, and chains connect the cuffs around her wrists and ankles. She is looking into Karen's eyes. "Oh God," she says. "Oh God, Karen."

Karen sticks her hand outside her cell, and Jackie grabs on. "Hey now," says one guard, and then another says, "Let her be, Joe."

"You will be clean," says Karen, quietly. "You'll start over."

"I will?" says Jackie.

"Yes," says Karen. "Don't be afraid." Jackie's hand is cold. After a long moment, she lets go.

By now, everyone is awake. Even the guards seem nervous; they do not stop Jackie when she tries to say goodbye. She starts with Sharleen, "Goodbye, Satan Killer." Sharleen does not look up, but closes her eyes, and nods.

Jackie moves on to Tiffany. "You'll get out of here. You're innocent, right?"

"Right," says Tiffany. She reaches between the bars to touch Jackie's hand. "I shouldn't have let you win that last Go Fish," she says. Jackie laughs weakly.

Veronica sticks her face right up to the bars and kisses Jackie's forehead. "Bless you, honey," she says.

Jackie comes back to Karen. "I'll start over?" she says.

"Yes," says Karen. "Don't be afraid."

"Come on," says the guard quietly. "It's time," he says. Jackie nods, and heads to the door. Keys rattle, the slide of the bars, footsteps. "Goodbye!" cries Jackie, and she is gone.

With a whoosh of applause, the TV comes on. "And how are you this morning, Kathie Lee?" says Regis Philbin.

The hours of Jackie's dying day pass slowly. The sewing machines hum as Veronica and Tiffany work. They are only allowed to watch the channels that do not talk about Jackie. Karen cannot read. She cannot think. She watches the ceiling of her cell. If she watches long enough, the cracks become pictures, monsters, animals. Everyone is quiet, even Sharleen. Lunch is tuna sandwiches and chocolate bars, a treat, as if they would trade Jackie, mean as she is, for a candy bar.

The mail comes at noon, but Karen never gets any mail. When the guard stops outside her door, Karen thinks it is time for a search, and holds out her hands for the circles of metal. Instead, a letter is slipped into her cell. Karen picks it up with trembling fingers.

The letter is light, and has been opened by the guards: a neat razor cut across the top of the envelope. The paper is very white. Karen holds it to her nose, but it does not smell of anything. There is no return address. The postmark says AUSTIN, TX.

Carefully, she slides the sheet of paper out of the envelope, and unfolds it. The handwriting is sloped and neat:

To Ms. Lowens,

I cannot believe that if I write this letter, and put it in the mail, it will reach your hands. What do your hands look like? I never looked at them in the trial. Do you bite your nails?

Henry used to bite his nails. He was my husband. He used to nick himself when he shaved, and crawl around on all fours to play with the dog, and bring me coffee in bed. He loved old music, and gardening, especially tomatoes. He loved cold beer, and fishing, and me.

I want you to understand what you did. When I wake up, and go to work, and come home, and eat dinner alone in front of the television, I want you to know that you took my life away. I don't know if you are sorry, or if you even care. I don't know if you want forgiveness, but you will never have it. I can never forgive you, and you have also done this: you have made me into someone who is filled with hate.

My mother tells me that this will get easier. It has been five years. Every night, I dread the morning.

Mrs. Henry Mills

Karen reads the letter, imagining the beautiful woman, Celia. Does she know that Karen watched her husband die? Would it help her to know? Karen waits for the guilt. She waits to feel sorry, to yearn for forgiveness. She waits, but nothing comes. It is too late, and she is tired. She is ready to leave this world.

franny

Death Row did not look the way Franny had expected it to. For one thing, there was the television, which was so loud Franny had to fight the urge to cover her ears: BUT BILLY IS DEAD, HOW CAN HE POSSIBLY BE THE FATHER OF YOUR CHILD, VIRGINIA? WELL, DARREN, THERE ARE THINGS YOU DON'T WANT TO KNOW…

In front of the television (WHAT ARE YOU TELLING ME, VIRGINIA? JUST SPIT IT OUT, DAMN YOU!), there was a metal table screwed to the floor, with chairs around it. On the table was a pack of cards and a magazine: *Quilting for Beginners.*

The floor was concrete, with a large, rusty drain in the middle. And the smell! It was different from the smell in the rest of the prison. It had a bitter, sour edge with no reassuring antiseptic. Underneath the screaming television (YOU DON'T WANT TO KNOW ABOUT BILLY, I SWEAR YOU DON'T! DON'T MAKE ME TELL YOU!), Franny could hear a river of small sighs, moans, and breathing.

Behind the concrete area were the cells. Franny knew that sometimes the women were allowed into the common area, but they were locked up during Franny's visit. Hamm, who had been chosen to give Franny her official tour, led Franny around, pointing out each woman. There was Sharleen, a huge black woman, her head thrown back, the hollow of her neck slick. Sharleen murmured in her sleep, and Franny saw the lurid paintings she had made on the walls of her cell, the chalk stars.

Next was Tiffany's cell (Franny could see shelves of makeup; Tiffany did not look up from her *People* magazine), and then Veronica's, covered with what looked like wedding photographs.

There was an empty cell next to Veronica's. The woman named Jackie had been taken to Huntsville, and her belongings had been removed.

The cell that held the woman from Uvalde, the woman named Karen, was last. She looked asleep when Franny stood before her cell; her breathing was steady and her eyes were closed. On her bed was a copy of *One Hundred Years of Solitude* and a letter. "This one here's got AIDS. She's got it bad," said Hamm.

Karen opened her eyes. From her wasted face, they shone, twin orbs of green fire. Orange around the pupils. Anna's eyes.

Franny gasped. "You OK there, Doc?" said Hamm, and Franny steadied herself.

"Yes," she said. "Yes, of course."

When Karen looked at her, Franny felt exposed and

frightened. She tried to imagine a life with nothing, and nothing to lose.

She tried to look at Karen with a clinical eye. Karen was in bad shape, and needed to be started on a stronger drug regimen immediately. Franny made a mental note to ask about her T-cell count. Karen's weight loss was evident in her sunken cheekbones.

She watched Franny steadily. Franny could see the little girl in front of the trailer, the small child Karen had been. Franny did not look away. She felt an unidentifiable emotion; a mixture of panic and anticipation.

"Hi," said Karen.

"Hi," said Franny.

"Well, that'll be all," said Hamm, taking Franny's elbow. Franny wanted to say something to the woman with Anna's eyes, something soothing—*I can save you*—but she was silent. As Hamm led her to the exit, Franny heard scraping metal and locks turning. Footsteps rang along the hallway, coming toward them.

Bars slid aside, and Janice Gaddon appeared. She looked exhausted, but her face was composed. She ignored Franny, faced the prisoners. She put her hands on her hips, and Franny saw her features harden. Inside the prison, Janice was so different from the woman who had sat barefoot under the stars, drinking wine and telling stories.

All of the prisoners stood up, and some held the bars for support. "Jackie Ford was executed at eleven-fifteen this morning," said Janice. One of the women, the blonde one named Tiffany, began to wail. Karen sank back to her bed and covered her face with her hands. The older woman, the Black Widow, pressed her eyes shut, and her body began to shake. Grasping the bars of her cell, her fingers grew red. Only Sharleen, on the far end, remained still.

Janice opened her mouth, but then closed it. She looked at the floor. "Are there any questions?" she said finally, in a tight but even voice.

There were no questions.

celia

Wherever I go, I see him out of the corner of my eye. This is not something I mention to anyone. At the supermarket, I will see a man in a suit holding a melon, and he will turn and he will be Henry. I know that Henry is dead, and I know that he did not like melons, never wore a suit, but I see his face, and I have to bite my tongue to keep from calling out.

I want to be rid of the memories. Sometimes, I wish I had never met Henry in the first place, never let him convince me to fly to Vegas on a two-for-one Southwest Airlines deal. How could I not have known, as I held his hand in the Elvis chapel? How could I have stood there in a satin dress, my hair piled on my head, and not seen what was coming? I ate the cake with my hands, letting Henry lick the frosting off my fingers.

If I had never met Henry, I would not have known those mornings in bed, with pages of the paper spread out, Henry's head bent, the sheets like waves around us. I would not have had that night on the Riverwalk in San Antonio, eating seafood pasta by candlelight, listening to Henry's story about the way he loved a girl in kindergarten so much that he snuck into the coatroom and kissed her coat every morning. I would not have felt Henry fill me.

Is it worth it? Sometimes I wonder. If I had never been filled by Henry, I would not be so empty now.

karen

There is so much time in Karen's day. She wants to put the letter out of her mind, but she cannot. After a few days, she decides to write back to Celia Mills, and calls her first meeting at the patio to explain the situation. "I don't know what to write to her," says Karen.

"Shit," says Tiffany. "That's a toughie, hon." Tiffany has gone to the Medical Center to have her blood tested for the DNA trial, and she has a Band-Aid in the crook of her arm.

"Why?" says Veronica. "That's what I'd like to know. Why do you want to write to this woman? Why now, after all of this time?"

Karen takes the letter out of its envelope, and presses it flat on the table. "What's that?" yells Sharleen from her cell.

"Come and see for yourself, Sharleen," says Tiffany. Sharleen makes a dismissive sound. Veronica rolls her eyes. But then, for the first time, Sharleen comes toward them. She sinks down into a chair. It is Jackie's chair.

"Let me see," she says. She grabs the letter, and looks at it.

"I want her to go on with her life, I guess," says Karen.

"You want to feel better about your own self," says Veronica. "Before you go to God."

There is a silence, and then Tiffany stands up from the table. "I have a headache," she says, walking to her cell.

"Girl, you are acting weird," says Sharleen.

"Let the woman hate you," says Veronica to Karen. "Don't write to her. Leave it alone."

"I saw him die," says Karen. "Her husband."

"And what good is that going to do her?" says Sharleen.

"No good," says Karen. "No good at all." She folds the sheet of paper and puts it back inside its envelope.

That night, they gather for the radio show, and of course Dan calls in first. His voice is scratchy, like wool. Tiffany stays in her cell, but looks up when she hears his voice.

"Hi, honey," says Dan. "I hope you're listening to me. We should know about the DNA in a week or two. Honey, Bob says we should really be able to use this in the appeal. You'll be home soon." His voice breaks. "Next to me," he says. Karen looks at Tiffany's eyes. They are dry.

"You better hope you innocent," says Sharleen, who is sitting in Jackie's chair again. Tiffany does not answer.

They have become separated: Tiffany and Veronica on one side, with their hopes and plans, and Sharleen and Karen on the other. Karen does not want to be on Sharleen's side.

franny

Franny fell into a pattern quickly, and the days passed. She woke, made coffee, drove to the prison listening to country hits in the Cadillac. All day, she drew blood and administered medications. The women's faces blended together. Franny was careful not to get to know them.

The only inmate Franny sought out was Karen. Her T-cell count was very low, but Franny hoped that with careful medication she could get better. Franny called Karen into the Medical Center often, and monitored her carefully. Once in a while, they spoke, reaching toward each other with words. Franny asked Karen about her life on Death Row, and Karen answered in a low murmur, telling Franny that she closed her eyes, let go of time, and let hours slip by. Karen told Franny about making tea with the hot coil, and about the Halloween party they had had the previous fall, when Jackie had cut Little Debbie cakes into tiny pieces, to make them last. When Karen spoke of Jackie, her voice fell to a whisper, as if in reverence.

At the end of the day, Franny drove. She drove on the highway sometimes, and sometimes on small back roads. The countryside soothed her, and she even grew to like Uncle Jack's car, which floated atop the road like a boat. The car was a cool haven in the summer heat. Franny sang along with Reba McEntire and Garth Brooks. The flat, parched land on either side made sense to her. There was rarely anyone outside.

On most evenings, she drank wine to try to ignore the loneliness that surrounded her. Magazines arrived addressed to Uncle Jack, and the contents of the kitchen drawers told his story: a book of matches from a restaurant in Waco; rubber bands carefully wound into a ball. Franny talked to him. *I am carrying on your work,* she told him, hoping somehow that driving to the prison each morning would help make up for the calls she had never returned, the things she had left unsaid.

Jed Lewis, after approving Franny's leave, had picked up Franny's belongings and shipped them to Texas, even finding an airline that would transport a cat. When Franny opened her boxes—Nat had thrown her clothes in haphazardly—she found a letter from Anna's father, asking her to stay in touch. She called the Gillisons' house one night, sitting in Uncle Jack's living room with her cat and a half-empty bottle of wine. When Mr. Gillison answered, however, Franny realized she had nothing to say, and hung up the phone.

She went to the Motor Inn Lounge occasionally, but it was usually empty, and Fred would watch television and ignore her. Franny didn't have the heart to clean the house; pizza boxes and dirty wine glasses piled up. After seeing Karen's copy of *One Hundred Years of Solitude*, Franny checked it out of the library. But even reading, her favorite escape, failed her: the words swam on the page, devoid of meaning. Late at night, instead of sleeping, Franny stared into the darkness and wished she believed in God.

She was gazing out her window one night when the phone rang. She took a sip of her wine. Who could possibly be calling her? She picked up the receiver.

"Dr. Wren? Franny Wren?" It was a man's voice, deep, wheezy.

"Yes?"

"This is Rick Underwood. I'm a defense lawyer."

Franny rolled her eyes. "What can I do for you, Mr. Underwood?"

"Rick, please."

"What can I do for you, Rick?"

"I know you must be very busy. But I need to speak to you. It's regarding one of my clients, Karen Lowens. I believe you've been treating her. By any chance, do you have time…for dinner? A drink?"

"I don't know…"

"I won't take much of your time."

"I'm free right now," said Franny, surprising herself.

"Now?"

"Well, or if you'd like…"

"No! No, Dr. Wren, now is fine."

"You can call me Franny."

"Franny. OK, Franny, how about some dinner? Have you been to Andy's Home Cookin'?"

"I have."

"Well, OK then. A half hour? I'm not far from Andy's. I'm staying at the Gatestown Motor Inn. Can I pick you up?"

"No," said Franny. "I'll see you there."

"Great. I'll be waiting outside."

"Okay." Franny hung up the phone. When she looked in the mirror, she realized her hair was oily and lank. As the bathtub filled, she sat on Uncle Jack's toilet seat, her chin in her hands. The bathroom badly needed cleaning, but the effort required to buy Ajax, sponges, brushes…it was just too much. One ratty towel hung from the towel rack. When she went to shave her legs, Franny found that her razor was rusty.

As she pulled into Andy's, Franny saw Rick waiting by the entrance. He was undoubtedly the worst dresser she had ever seen. He wore a mustard-yellow jacket with a blue shirt and a string tie. Holding up Wrangler jeans was a leather belt with an astonishingly hideous buckle featuring a longhorn bull. Rick took a drag of his cigarette, then dropped it to the pavement and ground it out with the heel of his boot. He looked less like a lawyer than he did a Bible salesman. Franny stepped from her car and Rick smiled uneasily. His smile, one bottom tooth crooked.

"Hello," said Franny, holding out her hand. Rick's grip was strong. The smell of his skin: clove, salt, fire.

"Thanks for coming," he said.

"It's fine," said Franny. "Really."

"It's just..." Rick shook his head. "Anyway," he said, holding open the door. As they waited for the hostess to seat them, Rick said, "Not a whole lot of people go out of their way."

Franny laughed, and Rick looked surprised. "That's the understatement of the year," she said. He shrugged, seeming uncomfortable with the bite in her voice.

On the bulletin board, there were pictures of horses, dogs, trucks, and guns for sale. And in the corner, a new, lavender flyer: YOGA WITH YOLANDA! SUPER STRESS RELIEF! WEDNESDAYS AT SIX, BASEMENT OF ST. DAVID'S!

"Right this way," said the hostess. She led them to a vinyl booth.

Rick ordered the Spaghetti Special with extra garlic breadsticks. Franny had the same. The televisions were turned off, and Franny could hear the conversation at the next table. "I can't believe I'm hearing this," said a man.

"Believe it, buddy," said a woman.

The late dinner crowd at Andy's was subdued, mostly tables of two. The fluorescent bulbs illuminated the dining room with such bright light that Franny felt as if she were in a school cafeteria. From hidden speakers, Barry Manilow crooned: *Her name was Lola. She was a showgirl. With yellow feathers in her hair and a dress cut down to there...*

"What you're doing over at the prison, Dr. Wren," said Rick, "well, I think it's a great thing."

"Thanks," said Franny. "Are you in private practice?"

"No. I'm one of the court-appointed attorneys. I get the real grisly stuff."

"Like Karen."

Rick nodded. "You've gotten to know her?"

Franny lifted her shoulders. "Some," she said. "I've been trying to help with the AIDS-related symptoms. She's pretty far gone, I'm sorry to say. I'm starting her on a new drug regimen, though. Just in case."

Rick's eyes were a light brown. "Why?" he said.

His gaze made Franny nervous. "Well, it just seems like the right thing to do," she said. She picked up her fork, then put it down.

From the next booth, the woman said, "You can *have* the dog, Jim."

"Anyway," said Franny. "Is that all you needed to discuss with me?"

"Well, Karen's had a hard time," said Rick. "I'm not sure how much you know about her life."

"Not much."

Their salads arrived, and as Franny speared wilted lettuce, Rick told her many of the facts she already knew from the gory library book: the rural childhood, the prostitution, the murders committed in self-defense.

"And you truly believe they were self-defense?" said Franny.

"Well," said Rick, "I'm not going to lie to you. She took these fellows' jewelry, their money, gave it to her junkie girlfriend. But she had been beat up pretty badly at some point. The examining doctors found scars from stab wounds, tears in her vagina and anus. Certainly, there's evidence that her accounts of the murders could be true. And, again, she had the opportunity to kill hundreds of men. She claims she only shot in self-defense. But then there's Henry Mills. He was a young guy, walked into a convenience store to get some groceries...Karen had just shot a john. It was the wrong place at the wrong time, I guess. He left a young widow." Rick sighed, stared into space for a moment. "But Karen didn't seem to get any thrill from the murders, the way your typical serial killer would."

"Your typical serial killer," said Franny. "Jesus."

Rick took his last bite of salad and picked up his napkin. "I represent several," he said, shaking his head. "How I ended up in my life I don't know. Sometimes I just can't believe it."

"I feel exactly the same way," said Franny. "Just today I was wondering what the hell I was doing in Gatestown."

"Having a Spaghetti Special," said Rick, as the waitress set the steaming plates down. He lifted his beer, and Franny touched her glass to his.

"To Gatestown," said Rick.

They ate in silence for a few minutes, and then Rick spoke. "For whatever reason, Dr. Wren, Karen tells me she feels close to you."

Franny looked up. "Really?" she said.

"Yes. I think you may be one of the few people who speaks with her at all."

"Rick, what do you need from me? Is there going to be another trial for Karen?"

Rick sipped his beer, and appeared to be choosing his words. "No. To answer your question, no, there's not going to be another trial. But there is one appeal left to keep Karen from being executed."

"And do you have high hopes?"

"Well, no. The governor, he's not too sympathetic. But that's where you come in. I was hoping you'd be a character witness for Karen. Just write a letter. It's a shot in the dark, I know. But if the governor doesn't change his mind, Karen will be executed on August twenty-fifth."

"I know," said Franny.

"I just thought I'd tell you," said Rick. "And, well, I was hoping that maybe you'd try to help."

"Oh, I don't know, Rick. I'm not the jury. I mean, it's not my place."

"Just think about it," said Rick.

"To be honest," said Franny, "I don't know if the AIDS won't kill her first."

"Maybe that would be a blessing," said Rick. He leaned in close to Franny, and she could smell him, his skin. "Will you think about it?" he said. "Writing a letter to the governor?"

"Sure," said Franny.

"That's all I ask," said Rick. When the check came, he paid it.

celia

Surprisingly, things at the library remained much the same as they had been before I took a young lover into my bed. I received no sly glances, no comments, and there seemed to be no heat or sex vibes exuding from me. Even Harriet Peabody, a hippie-turned-aqua-aerobics-instructor who checks out books like *Harnessing Your Psychic Self* and *Crystal Ball Creativity*, walked by me without a glance. (She had come in to see if we had received the new issue of *Cat Fancy*; we had not.) I must admit, it was a bit disappointing.

Marc had not called, and I was glad. Although an orgasm with a young stud was fabulous in its own way, I really wasn't prepared to date a man who could not buy wine on the way over for dinner. Also, the charm of a struggling artist wears off fast. I know: Henry had wanted to be a composer, but had become a Java programmer instead. Those long nights, those conversations in which Henry had strummed his guitar and started in with the *I have given up on my dreams*. . . . Honestly, I couldn't go through that again.

However, my sexual appetite seems to have reawakened. I find myself checking out patrons as they are checking out books. Good old Charles, who reads all the weepy women's novels, suddenly seems attractive in his hospital scrubs. Ken Mendel, who's been writing a book about the history of golf for years, seems less a drunken freak and more a possible afternoon liaison. Even Abe, I have to admit, looks pretty good for eighty. (I will note here that I have *not* checked out young Finnegan for even *one second*.)

What to do? I am a horny widow, not something I'm thrilled about being. In my evening appointment with Maureen, she told me to take it one day at a time.

"Oh, Maureen," I said, jamming my mouth full of jellybeans from the bowl she keeps on her desk, "how else would I take it? I mean, really." Maureen, a bit snide but a good person at heart, admitted that I had a point.

Geraldine Flat comes straight from Huntsville to my desk at the library. "What?" I say to Geraldine. She looks terrible. She has circles under her eyes, and her hair looks like a bird's nest (one of my mother's favorite expressions, and very applicable in this circumstance).

"I have been," says Geraldine, pausing dramatically, "at an all-night vigil protesting the death penalty."

I sigh. She is blocking my view of the hot new lawyer in town, who is flipping through the *Readers' Guide to Periodical Literature*.

"They killed Jackie Ford," Geraldine says, letting her shoulders slump forward. "And Karen Lowens is next."

I begin to laugh. I can't help it. The thought of Geraldine Flat, poking a cardboard sign in the air, surrounded by eighteen-year-olds, well, it's just too much. "Are you laughing?" says Geraldine Flat.

"Oh, Geraldine," I say, "Why don't you fuck off?"

karen

Karen's visits to Dr. Wren are the highlight of her day. Although she feels weak most of the time—the nausea is constant now, a sickening weight, and her pneumonia makes it hard to breathe—her visits to the clinic are peaceful and quiet. Karen thinks constantly about Dr. Wren's small earlobes, her perfume smell, her long white teeth.

In the Medical Center, Dr. Wren slides a syringe into Karen's arm. Karen remembers Ellen sliding the needle in. Karen will have the same track marks.

Karen can feel it: she is dying. She has to fight for breath, and even the sedative does not quell her panic. Dr. Wren is looking out the window. There is only a concrete wall there. Karen opens her mouth. "I don't want it to be this way," she says.

Dr. Wren turns; the light from the window makes a line on her face. "What?"

"I don't want to die choking."

Dr. Wren is silent, and then she comes and sits next to

Karen. She touches Karen's hand, and looks into her eyes. "Does it matter how you die, do you think?"

"It matters to me," says Karen.

And it does matter, a great deal. Karen has begun talking to God in her cell at night, and God has given her visions. Karen sees her body, giving up its soul. A clean break is the best way; struggling for breath will cut her to pieces. She also has a vision where her soul rises (in these dreams, her soul is smoky, glowing, and the body it leaves behind is brittle and dry) but Dr. Wren runs after it, jumping and grabbing bits to bring them back, trying to press them inside the shell on the table. In the vision, Dr. Wren will not let Karen's smooth soul escape.

"Do you think the morphine tablets are helping you?" says Dr. Wren. Karen shrugs. The pain is constant, gnawing. "We can put you on a drip," says Dr. Wren. She points to the machine in the corner of the room, a bright cylinder.

"I don't know."

"You'd have the IV in all the time," says Dr. Wren. "And you could give yourself morphine when you needed it, just by pushing a button."

Karen stares at the white canister, the tubes snaking from it like arms. "Could I give myself enough to die?" she says.

"What?" Dr. Wren's eyes narrow.

"I'm just joking," says Karen. But she is thinking about how it would feel, the warmth spreading through every limb, morphine filling her veins. The noise, the guards, the pain fading away, and God opening His arms to hold her.

"I'd program the machine, limiting the amount you could administer, of course," says Dr. Wren. From her lab coat she pulls out a small, red notebook. "I've got the code to the machine in here," she says. "And I'd make sure you only had what you needed."

"Not yet," says Karen.

Dr. Wren looks at her notebook, and puts it away. In the corner, the machine waits.

Later, as the guards lead Karen back through the screams and the banging metal, she pretends she can still smell Dr. Wren. Dr. Wren seems so young, and so nervous. Ellen was like that, back before everything went wrong.

It is not that Karen loves the doctor. It is just that Dr. Wren is empty, without faith. Maybe, Karen thinks, she can help her somehow, take care of her the way she took care of Ellen. Karen is tired of having nobody.

franny

When Franny left the prison Tuesday evening, she tilted her head to the sun, and took a long breath, smelling the grass. She felt like crying with the joy of it.

The big news in the prison that week was the Black Widow's wedding. This woman had married seven husbands, and now she was engaged again. Karen had told Franny that Veronica was a kind person, that she really loved this new fiancé, Jimmy. Franny had a hard time believing it.

On Friday, Veronica's wedding day, Franny woke early. As she showered, she felt giddy, as if it were prom night. She dressed in a gray suit (she had not worn anything other than cotton slacks in days, and her pumps felt strange now that her feet were used to sneakers) and applied lipstick. She had run out of her expensive New York shampoo and used bars of soap instead. She had stopped using her hair dryer, usually pulled her hair back in the rubber band from the morning paper, the *Gatestown Messenger*. Dark clouds rolled across the sky, and it began to rain as Franny drove to the prison.

"I can see you dressed up for the wedding," said Deborah, pouring coffee in the Medical Center.

"Oh, is that today?" said Franny.

Deborah put her hands on her hips. "You know it is," she said. Deborah was round and small, and there was something strange about the way she acted around Franny, something in her tone. She treated Franny like a wayward teenager.

The morning was filled with flu shots and a woman whose eye had been punched almost out of the socket. "That fucking bitch," said the woman, who was skinny with pigtails. Franny tended to the wound, and did not say a word. "She fucking jumped me," said the woman. "In the fucking shower. Bullshit." Franny did not respond.

The wedding was planned for visiting hours. Veronica would have to be handcuffed throughout. She and her new husband would not be granted conjugal visits.

At four, Deborah came into the clinic. "Are you coming, Franny?" she said.

"No, I'm too busy, thanks."

"There aren't so many good things here," said Deborah. She looked as if she wanted to say more, but Franny had bent her head to write notes. "Laceration above and below brow," she wrote. Finally, Deborah left.

Franny decided to make a pot of coffee. She dumped the morning's coffee in the sink, and got a new filter from the cupboard. *Who would marry a woman on Death Row?* she wondered. *A sixty-year-old woman who had killed seven husbands before?* Franny could imagine presenting the case before her psych class in med school. Her classmates would furrow their brows, ask questions in bewildered voices: Did the man believe Veronica was innocent? Didn't he know she'd never be free? Did he have a death wish, do you think?

When her mug was full, Franny took a sip, and then put it down. She just had to see the ceremony. Franny walked quickly down the hallway to the visiting room.

"Going to the chapel and she's gonna get maaaaried..." sang a voice. Franny hurried along, her head down. She hated the way the inmates yelled coarsely, insultingly, incessantly. At the window to the visiting room, she stopped.

The room was filled. There were people on both sides of the glass wall that separated the guests from the prisoners. Guards surrounded Veronica, some smiling, some watching passively. Visitors and staff stood on the other side of the glass. Some of them looked a bit like Veronica—daughters, maybe, sons. Some cradled babies in their arms, and there were children—children!—in frilly dresses and pressed pants. Franny shook her head.

In the front of the room, the chaplain, a mousy woman named Moira, read from her Bible. Moira held a telephone mouthpiece, so that Jimmy, on the other side of the glass, could hear. Veronica wore a long, white gown. (She had ordered the dress from a discount bridal catalog, Karen had divulged. Veronica's gray hair was covered with a sheet, trailing behind her to the floor. She was made up like a showgirl: bright lipstick and rouge.

The husband had to be twenty years younger than Veronica. He was bone-thin with dark hair and a dark complexion. He stood proudly, holding the receiver to his ear. Through the glass, he gazed at Veronica.

Franny squeezed into the visiting room. The door closed with a bang, and everyone turned around. Franny stared into her coffee. The chaplain looked up, but then resumed reading into the mouthpiece. Jimmy began his vows, speaking quietly and forcefully. Franny could not help feeling a shiver when he said, so seriously, "until death do us part."

As Jimmy spoke, Franny looked at Veronica's face. It was clear, shining, and something inside Franny melted. She forgot the circumstances, just for that flickering moment, and she saw two people in love.

After the ceremony, the guards led Veronica away, and her new husband watched her go. He was hugged by his relatives, and a baby started crying. There were no pictures, no flowers, no music. When everyone had left, Franny went to pick up a gum wrapper on the floor.

"Franny, how are you doing?" Franny stood quickly, and turned around. Deborah was in the middle of the room. "I mean, really," said Deborah.

"I'm fine," said Franny, but she suddenly felt tired. "It's just so sad," she said. Deborah came forward, put her hand on Franny's arm.

"Jack told me you kept it all inside," said Deborah, and then she stopped.

"What?" said Franny. "Did you say Jack?"

"I didn't…" said Deborah.

"He told you about me?" said Franny, incredulous. But as she looked at Deborah, it fell into place. "You and Uncle Jack," she said. "Of course."

Deborah did not answer, but did not look away. Finally, she said, "I didn't know how to tell you. I guess I was afraid you'd be hurt, or something."

"No," said Franny, "I'm glad." They stood in the room, the remnants of the wedding around them, and Franny said, "I drank your Tab."

Deborah smiled. "It's fine," she said.

Franny looked at the scuffed floor, covered in muddy footprints of all sizes. There was so much mud. The room was a mess, littered with wrappers and rice that guests had thrown on Jimmy. Even Uncle Jack had shared his life. There were a hundred breaths filling the room, pressing in on Franny. Inside her, there was nothing.

Let's be honest. There were nights when Franny got drunk. She sat in her old room at Uncle Jack's house and drank until things seemed loose and even funny. Usually, it was the cheap wine from the Spurs Gas Mart, but sometimes it was beer or whiskey. She got drunk. And then she called people and hung up. She called college friends, she called Nat's mother, she called her old number in New York to hear the answering machine. (Nat had changed the message, of course, and now it said, *It's Nat. You know what to do.*) Once, she called Christopher, the Houston newscaster she had met at the Motor Inn Lounge.

She would listen to the ringing phones, hear the pause after people had waked and picked up, but before they remembered where they were, or what to say. She listened to the hesitant "Hello?" The second, puzzled, "Hel-*lo*?" and the various curses: "Asshole!" "Hello? Hello? Fucker!" Nat's mother hung up after the second hello. When Franny ran out of familiar numbers, she would just dial, to see what happened. Nothing much happened.

She watched ants. There were ants in her room, and they climbed up the wall. The amazing thing, she thought, was that the ants followed each other's trails. It was as if they knew where the previous ants had been. Perhaps they left an invisible scent? They climbed up the wall by Franny's bed, and then into one of the crevices. Franny tried not to leave food out, but she forgot, and the ants came, and Franny watched them.

At the request of Tiffany's lawyer, Franny had taken a blood sample from Tiffany for DNA testing. Tiffany had been pale and quiet when Franny had inserted the needle. Franny sent the blood to Dallas to be analyzed at the same lab where the skin underneath the twins' fingernails was being tested. Some of the nurses in the Medical Center had opinions about Tiffany's innocence, but Franny stayed clear of their discussions. While Franny was drawing Tiffany's blood, Tiffany bit her lip. When it was over, she said "Thank you" in a voice as sweet as candy.

◆ ◆ ◆

On Wednesday evening, Franny went to the Gatestown Public Library, and looked up old newspaper stories about Tiffany. The old men no longer stared when Franny came inside, simply nodded.

According to the papers, Tiffany had been brought up as a Dallas socialite. There was a picture of her as the Homecoming Queen at her prep school, Ravenwood. She was standing in front of a football player, his thick arms around her hips. Her smile was wide and joyless.

There was no evidence of abuse, although one childhood friend (now the wife of an oil executive in Midland, Texas) claimed Tiffany had said she'd learned everything there was to learn about sex from her father, an Exxon landman. In the pictures, Tiffany's father was tan and arrogant-looking. His wife, Tiffany's mother, was thin as a whisper. Her name was Sissy.

Tiffany went on to become a cheerleader at the University of Texas, and surprised everyone when she married a computer designer, Dan Brooks. Dan was short and wore glasses. He founded Brooks Solutions, and sold his output management software for millions. The couple lived in a sprawling mansion on the outskirts of Houston (their house looked like a Tuscan villa), and had twin girls, Joanna and Josie. In the backyard there was a large pond.

Dan, who became a freelance software consultant, traveled often, leaving his family alone in their giant house.

A neighbor, a dog groomer named Doris, claimed that Tiffany suffered from depression, and on one occasion locked her two daughters in the yard. "They ran around naked as jaybirds, and who knows where Miss Cheerleader was," said Doris. Tiffany, according to Doris, "took a lot of naps."

But many other neighbors called Tiffany "an ideal mother," "a real sweetheart," and "someone who does the baking cookies thing." She seemed to be well-liked at the twins' nursery school, where she volunteered as a Reading Buddy. "She was a hottie," confided one local teen.

At a ballet recital, according to Madame Clouchet, a Houston teacher, Tiffany arrived in a leotard and tutu that matched her four-year-old daughters'. This, said Madame Clouchet, "was a bit, how you say, bizarre."

On September twenty-fourth, 1991, Tiffany and Dan hired a babysitter, Laura Volman, and went to dinner at Goode's Seafood. Dan ordered the mesquite catfish and two Shiner beers, Tiffany a side salad with lite vinaigrette and a glass of white zinfandel. Their waitress, Shirley Smith, says they "were real nice, whatever, you know, it was busy." Dan paid in cash.

After returning home, Dan drove the babysitter to her house. "He gave me twenty bucks. They always paid well, because they were rich," said Laura. Laura had played Barbie with the twins, and then turned on the television. "I was supposed to, like, read to them, but 'Beverly Hills 90210' was on," said Laura.

Dan had gone to bed upstairs. He left Tiffany and the twins watching a Disney movie in the TV room downstairs. He thinks the movie had an elephant in it.

At three-twenty a.m. on September twenty-fifth, Tiffany called 9-1-1 in hysterics. The conversation was reported in a *Houston Chronicle* article:

9-1-1, how can I help you?

Hello? Hello?

Ma'am, how can I help you?

My babies! My babies! They're gone, my babies!

Ma'am, can you give me your name?

They're gone! Help, oh my God…

Please calm down, ma'am.

Calm down? Calm down? Oh, my God! Oh, my God!

Please give me your name.

*Tiffany Brooks. Oak Spring Road. Tiffany Brooks, oh my
God…*

Ma'am, do you need an ambulance?

*No, no, they're gone! Somebody kidnapped my babies! I
don't know…*

What happened?

*I was asleep. I fell asleep, I woke up, there was a man, and
now they're gone! Someone came in my house…my babies,
help me!*

Ma'am, what is your exact address?

*I found a knife…I'm hurt. I picked it up. Oh no, I ruined the
fingerprints! Oh, God, help me!*

According to Tiffany, she had fallen asleep in front of
the television with the twins. The next thing she remembers
is Josie calling her. She heard Josie saying, "Mommy!" She
recounted the next few minutes in her court transcript:

*I heard Josie call me and I woke up. There was blood on my
shirt. It is very blurry, I can barely remember what happened
next. I called for Josie and Joanna. They did not answer me.*

They were not in the room. I heard footsteps in the kitchen. I ran into the kitchen. I saw the back of someone, a man. He ran out the door. He dropped a knife. I picked up the knife. I ran outside. There was nobody, no car. I screamed. I called 9-1-1.

Dan, according to his court transcript, woke when he heard Tiffany's screams:

I heard her screaming. She was screaming, "Oh my God." I got out of bed and ran downstairs. Tiffany was in the kitchen, and she was stabbed, she was bleeding and screaming. The back door was open. I ran outside, but I couldn't see anything. The twins were gone.

The ambulance arrived and took Tiffany to the emergency room. She had been stabbed in her chest and neck. The doctors concluded that the wounds were from a knife. The police ordered roadblocks and searched the neighborhood for Josie and Joanna. It was the next morning when, searching the grounds of the Brookses' home, a police officer found a small sock in the mud at the side of the pond. When the pond was searched, the bodies of Josie and Joanna were found. They both wore sleeping suits, which had been filled with rocks.

As the investigation wore on, Tiffany began to emerge as a suspect. Her stab wounds could have been self-inflicted, doctors determined, although one wound, on her right forearm, would have been very difficult for her to have caused. Also, Tiffany's behavior was deemed strange by psychologists—the mention of picking up the knife and the ruined fingerprints in her 9-1-1 call. Her story of a strange man running out the back door yielded no leads. A window screen had been slashed, but the dust on the windowsill beneath it had not been disturbed. No prints were found in the house and on the knife other than Tiffany's. Tiffany and her husband maintained their innocence.

"Why would I kill my babies?" Tiffany said to a reporter, crying. No answer to that question was ever found.

A jury convicted Tiffany Brooks of drowning her two daughters. She was sentenced to death.

Tiffany and Dan had been fighting to get the DNA under their daughters' fingernails examined for years when the approval finally came through. Whoever's skin was under the girls' nails was undoubtedly the person the girls had struggled with while being drowned. Only faint scratches were found on Tiffany, but much of her skin had been torn from the stabbing.

On Friday, the call came from Dallas. They had received the results of Tiffany's blood test, and compared it with the DNA in the tissue samples. Franny assured the lab that the sample had been Tiffany's blood, and they told her the results: the DNA samples were the same.

Yoga with Yolanda! Franny decided to go. She thought it was time for a little stress relief. Even after her running shoes had arrived from New York, she had barely used them. It was just too hot for exercise, and Franny felt sluggish and heavy.

On Wednesday night, she put on sweatpants and a T-shirt and walked to St. David's Catholic Church. It was on the corner of Main and Sixth, a brick building with high windows and a large, brass bell. By the time she arrived, she was about ten minutes late, and couldn't find the basement entrance. A woman came out the front door and folded her arms over her chest.

"Oh, hello," said Franny.

"You're stepping on the grass," said the woman. She had a pinched face, and wore an apron.

Franny looked down at the parched dirt underneath her sneakers. "I'm looking for yoga?" she said. When the woman did not respond, she said, "With Yolanda?"

"Yolanda Berks?" The woman's voice was skeptical.

"I'm not really sure. It's in the basement of St. David's?"

The woman did not uncross her arms. She sniffed. "Basement's down here," she said, pointing to some wooden stairs and stepping back for Franny to enter the front door. This woman could use some yoga, thought Franny.

The church smelled like cedar and incense. It was cool and dark, with candles flickering deep inside. Franny had been brought up without religion, but felt a sharp pang of yearning as she looked inside the church. How nice it would be, she thought, to believe someone else was in charge. Or, like Karen, to believe there was an escape in death. To believe that one could make a mistake and still be saved.

As Franny descended, each step creaked beneath her. The basement was a large, wood-paneled room filled with older women in leotards. They were bending, touching their toes, and Franny was confronted with at least ten women's bottoms. As they concentrated on stretching, the women's faces filled with blood, some bit their lips, their hair hung down. At the front of the room was the woman from the Gatestown Motor Inn Lounge, the piano player who drank martinis and slurred Broadway show tunes. "Focus on your chakra, feel it, feel it," she was saying.

The women groaned, their rumps shook, faces grew redder. Franny tried to turn her gaze away from them, but there was nothing else to see. Finally, the lounge singer said, "Release!" and they stood.

"Hello," she said, then, "I'm Yolanda. Welcome, new friend." Some women turned around, and Franny recognized Betty, the front desk clerk at the Motor Inn, and the librarian, Louise. Franny smiled nervously.

"New friend, look at your clothes," said Yolanda. "I cannot see your joints in those pants."

"I'm sorry," said Franny.

"Next time, a leotard!" said Yolanda, who sported an aqua one on her portly frame.

"I'm sorry," said Franny again.

"No matter," said Yolanda. "Grab a sticky mat." She gestured to a pile of rolled green mats at her side. Franny took one, and unrolled it in the very back row.

"New friend," said Yolanda. "Come to the front."

Franny sighed, and took her mat to the front.

"Now we down dog!" said Yolanda.

They stretched and flexed, obeying Yolanda's every command. As they held yoga poses, Yolanda walked among them, pushing on a hip here, steadying an arm there. By the end of the class, Franny felt wonderful, giddy and light.

"Now, it is time for rest," said Yolanda, and she handed out blankets and little beanbags.

The women stretched out on their mats, pulled up their blankets, and placed the beanbags over their eyes. Yolanda played a tape of sitar music. "You are letting go," said Yolanda. "Let go, from your toes to your head, and let your soul float to the stars."

On her thin mat, Franny closed her eyes. She relaxed her toes, knees, hips. By the time she had reached her shoulders, she smelled a lavender perfume, and felt Yolanda place a blanket on her, warming her.

That night, Franny dreamt of Nat. They were in their apartment, in the dark, dancing. Nat slipped his hand underneath her shirt, pressed his lips to hers. It was such a vivid dream—his breath hot against her ear, his sleepy smell, his palm touching her breast—that when she woke, she remembered how much she had once loved him, and before she could stop herself, her eyes were wet with tears.

celia

It seems that saying "fuck" to a patron is not acceptable librarian behavior. My supervisor, Kaytee, called me in for a chat. "Why don't you take a teensy vacation?" she said.

I looked at Kaytee, her fake blonde hair. "I don't have anywhere to go," I said.

"How about Florida?" she said brightly. "Florida is lovely this time of year."

"It's August," I said.

"Righty-o," said Kaytee. "How about Reno, Nevada?"

"How long?"

"Hm?"

"How long do you want me gone?" I said.

"How about a few weeks? Why don't you come back in September. Just take a nice break, Celia." She did not mention the execution of my husband's killer. "You just seem distracted," said Kaytee.

◆ ◆ ◆

I went home, and found a large manila envelope in my mailbox. The return address was Underwood & Associates. The name sounded familiar, but I couldn't place it. I thought of the hot new lawyer in town, but I knew in my heart that he had not sent me a manila envelope.

I pushed aside a pile of dirty plates, sank onto the couch, and opened the envelope. On top of a folder of Xerox copies was a note in a messy scrawl: *Dear Ms. Mills, Can you take mercy on Karen Lowens? Her execution is August 25th. A letter from you could save her life. Thank you for your time. Sincerely, Rick Underwood.*

You have got to be fucking kidding me is what I thought. But I kept reading. The first page was a doctor's examination notes: Karen's physical exam on the night she was arrested.

> *Karen Lowens, Black Female, DOB 07/03/68*
>
> *Patient highly agitated, Blood Alcohol Level 3.2*
>
> *Evidence of two (2) prior breaks in jawbone.*
>
> *Evidence of severe trauma to left eye. Patient claims her eye was "knocked out" by a male fist.*
>
> *Four (4) broken teeth (details in dental records).*
>
> *Neck shows evidence of recent bruising.*
>
> *Evidence of prior break in right collarbone.*
>
> *Evidence of prior breaks in three (3) ribs.*
>
> *Severe scarring in anus and buttocks, evidence of puncture wounds to anus.*

Severe scarring in vagina, several tears in vaginal wall, evidence of cigarette burns on vaginal wall.

Evidence of prior break in right ankle.

So Karen Lowens had been beaten up. I knew this information already, and I was not interested in thinking about it. Save her life! As if Henry had been given a chance to save his. I threw the package away and called my mother. My voice was trembling.

"Celia," she said, alarmed. "What is it?"

I told her everything: the boy-toy, swearing at Geraldine, the faux-vacation, the letter from Karen Lowens' lawyer. "Oh, sweetie," said my mother. "Oh, my sweet girl."

"How can they think I would write a letter for this woman?" I said.

My mother paused. "Listen," she said. "You listen to me, sweetie. I want you to call Maureen, and then I want you to go out and buy something nice for dinner. I'm coming to Texas, sweetie, just hang on."

"You don't have to come," I said.

"Don't be absurd," she said. "I'm calling the travel agent right now."

I did not call Maureen. I turned on the television, and I watched "Law & Order". I wondered: would Angie Harmon forgive a murderer? My mother called to say she was coming in three days, could I hang on? I said yes. I was not sure this was true.

◆ ◆ ◆

That night Henry came down to talk to me. I saw him on the end of my bedpost, and here is what he said: *Celia, let go.* He was wearing the Elvis T-shirt I had bought him in Graceland, on our honeymoon. *Write the letter,* he said, *do something good.*

He did not mention fucking the boy. I was relieved about that.

karen

On Saturday morning, Tiffany is given the results of the DNA test. The skin underneath her children's fingernails belongs to her. There is no evidence of foreign DNA. "I can't believe it!" says Tiffany, her eyes blazing. "It's just fucking ridiculous!" She is brushing her hair; it is visiting day. "How did that motherfucker do it? How did he drown the girls without getting any evidence on them?"

"Honey, I sure don't know," says Veronica. She is painting her nails, and gazing at her wedding ring finger, onto which she has drawn a red band with a permanent marker.

"I know," rasps Sharleen. "That motherfucker is you, you sick fuck." She laughs, a terrible sound.

"Shouldn't you be in hell by now?" says Tiffany, stepping outside her cell. Sharleen doesn't answer.

A guard raps on the metal, and Tiffany puts down her brush, smiling. "Veronica," says the guard. Veronica stands, and holds out her wrists. The television is loud, louder than ever.

"It's just so unfair!" says Tiffany, and then she says,

"Where is Dan?" She puts her hands on her hips. Her nails are painted Cotton Candy Pink.

Tiffany sits in front of the TV and waits. Through the hours of cartoons, she waits, tapping her tiny Ked. When she hears footsteps in the hallway, she jumps up, but the guard says, "Karen." Tiffany sits back down, a look of bewilderment on her face.

Rick is sitting in the green room. "No glass today," he says cheerfully when Karen enters. "I pulled some strings," he says. "So I hear you're getting state-of-the-art medical attention." Rick's chin is unshaven, grizzled. Karen nods.

"Still, you don't look so good."

Karen shrugs. "OK, sweetheart, let's get it going here. You want a cigarette?" He shakes one from the pack and lights it for Karen, handing it over. "Now I'll be honest with you," says Rick. "This governor, he's an asshole. We can't count on him for a ham sandwich, much less a pardon."

Karen is so tired. Her body is suffused with pain, as if it were liquid, filling her to the brim.

"We're going to have to give this everything we've got," Rick is saying. "Let me tell you what I'm thinking," he says.

The noise in the prison is worse and worse. The pepper spray, the vomit. The searches, tooth powder, television always blaring.

"I'm ready to die," says Karen.

Rick looks up from his notes. "I don't think you mean that. We've got an appeal left, honey."

Karen is silent. Rick runs his hand over the back of his

neck. "As I was saying," he says, and he goes on. Karen waits for him to be finished. She lets him say his piece. She thinks of Ellen kissing someone else. She thinks of her mother, shooting smack. She thinks of Tiffany, her matching DNA. But then she thinks of Dr. Wren, and her small bones. Dr. Wren's hand is as little as a bird's wing. Her wrist is the size of a kiss. She is so lonely, and so afraid. In the way that physical pain fills Karen, fear fills Dr. Wren. She starts at loud noises, gets nervous in close proximity. She waits for the worst, every minute. And she keeps fighting, refusing to accept God's plan. Refusing to just let go, give in, and open her heart. Yes, someone needs Karen in this world.

Rick goes on and on about clemency, the governor. When he is finished, and looking at her with sharp eyes, she speaks.

"Is there a chance?" she says. "Do I have a chance?"

"Yes," says Rick. He grabs her hand. "You have a chance, goddamn it," he says.

Karen nods, and then Rick hugs her. His arms are hot. His shoes make a banging sound as he walks down the hallway, and he swings his briefcase, full of the papers for her appeal.

Karen is brought back to her cell. Tiffany is still watching television, her eyes red. "Who's visiting *you*?" she says.

"My lawyer," says Karen.

And then the guard comes, footsteps, a key. "Finally!" says Tiffany. But it is not Dan. It is Veronica, coming back. Veronica looks surprised to see Tiffany in front of the TV, but does not say anything.

After a time, Tiffany goes back inside her cell.

Dan never comes. He never comes again.

As each day drags on, Karen waits with an intensity that is fierce. It is no longer idle waiting. Her life is finite. Each day is long, excruciatingly long, and filled with raw noise and pain. She vomits everything now, and has sores on her skin and lips. The drugs don't seem to do anything, and Karen is scared.

Finally, Karen asks Dr. Wren for the morphine machine. Dr. Wren connects Karen to the white canister, explaining each detail. Karen watches her carefully. "Now, I'm going to let you have a steady stream," says Dr. Wren, "and if you think you need more, let me know. We can up the dosage."

Karen nods.

Dr. Wren looks uncomfortable as she takes her red notebook from her coat. She checks the number of the machine, runs her finger down a page, and nods. "I'm going to have to ask you to turn away, Karen," she says. Karen is hurt, but closes her eyes. Dr. Wren punches in the code, beep, beep, beep, beep, beep, beep. "All done," she says.

"You don't trust me?" says Karen.

Dr. Wren sighs. She has already closed her notebook and tucked it safely away. "Morphine is a dangerous drug," she says.

"Oh yeah," says Karen, "I might die."

There are tears in Dr. Wren's eyes, but Karen ignores them.

◆　◆　◆

Tiffany has retreated to her cell. She writes long letters to Dan and the people who once supported her, but she does not get letters back. She still pores over the law books, but is just as likely to open a Bible. She is turning into a long-timer, her ties to the outside world weakening, retreating like tentacles. This is the way to live your life inside: forget the outside—the feel of rain, the joy of driving a car with choices about where to turn. Find someone to love inside the walls, stop waiting for your name on visiting day. It is easy, in some ways, like sinking into quicksand, or sadness. Just give up your grip.

Veronica refuses to forget the outside. Her new husband writes every day, and visits on weekends. Of course, he loves a ghost, an idea, and not the flesh-and-blood Veronica (Karen knows that Veronica snores in the middle of the night, and sucks her thumb when she thinks no one is looking, and Jimmy will never know these things), but Karen thinks this is the best kind of love. In fact, it is probably the only kind. When someone really knows you is when it all falls apart.

Sharleen sleeps most of the time. Periodically, she chants frightening things in her cell, or screams out in the night. It is hard to ignore her, but they try.

On Monday, Samantha Hawkins is convicted of dropping her son out of an apartment window. They watch her on the television news: a beautiful woman with long, dark hair. She wears bright lipstick, and has high cheekbones. Her baby died instantly when he hit the pavement. She went for the insanity plea, but was given the death penalty. The women on Death Row are excited, despite themselves, for her arrival. She is a pageant-winner, Miss Teen Texas.

They hear her before they see her. She sings as they lead her to Death Row: *Who will saaave your soul*…Even Sharleen looks dumbfounded. They all came in crying, slumped, terrified. And here is this Beauty Queen, headed toward them, singing a teen ballad. (They have been allowed to watch the Grammy Awards. Though they know little about answering machines, e-mail, or cell phones, they are quite up-to-date on pop culture.)

The gates slide back, and holding up two guards as if they were her dates to a debutante ball, Samantha waltzes in. "Hey girls!" she cries. She is whippet-thin, twenty years old, with thick, curled hair. She has big lips and eyebrows that are plucked in a perfect arc. Her round breasts jut out from her jumpsuit, which she has unbuttoned to show her impressive cleavage. Her eyes are glittery.

"You better shut up, honey," growls Sharleen. "If you know what's good for you."

"Well if it isn't the Satan Killer," says Samantha. "You look much cuter in person."

The guards grab Samantha roughly, and throw her into Jackie's cell. "Oh, goody," she says, looking up underneath her thick lashes. "Television all damn day." Her giggle is unnerving. When she was asked, in the beauty pageant, what the most important issue facing children in the world today is, she answered, "Life."

Karen tries to close her ears. She is too tired to listen to
the old courting routine. Everyone will want to be
Samantha's friend, or her worst enemy. Karen bets that
Tiffany will win Samantha, but she doesn't have the energy
to watch the games. Luckily, the drugs keep Karen from
staying awake for more than an hour at a stretch. She does
not fall into sleep, but has visions: Ellen, her mother, the
men she has killed. She cannot remember things, like what
day it is, or what television show comes on at three.

Karen lies in bed, and pushes the black morphine
button that brings her reprieve. She pushes it again and
again. She imagines Dr. Wren's boyish body, her slim hips
and flat breasts. Karen imagines cradling Dr. Wren in her
arms, her small head resting on Karen's rib cage. They are
not sexy visions. In them, Karen is not Dr. Wren's lover, but
her mother.

Rick Underwood calls every day, and they let Karen take
the calls. "I'm working on this," he says. He is writing letters,
talking to the radio and television. When the guards' attention
lapses, Karen sees Rick on the news, begging for mercy.

"This woman is dying of AIDS," he says. "And I beg the
governor of this great state to let her die in peace."

"Your T-cell is dropping," says Dr. Wren one afternoon.
"Will I be gone soon?" says Karen.

Dr. Wren sighs. "I'm not going to lie to you, Karen," she
says. She stands close. Karen can smell her, an almond
smell, a new kind of soap. Dr. Wren's hair has grown longer,

and her braid falls down her back. There is another smell, sharper. Karen breathes in. Booze. It is in Dr. Wren's skin.

"Look, it doesn't go uphill from here. But you still have time."

Karen laughs bitterly. She pushes the black button, and the warmth comes in a rush.

Dr. Wren looks at her, looks into her eyes, as if deciding something. Oh, if Karen could only kiss her, those thin lips, taste Dr. Wren. She would taste like celery.

"Karen," says Dr. Wren. "If you hold on…there are new drugs being researched…"

Karen nods.

"With these drugs," says Dr. Wren, "you could have…" Dr. Wren's voice fades as she says, "years."

Karen feels bile rise in her throat. "What do you know?" she says. "What do you know about my life?"

Dr. Wren is silent. "I don't," she says quietly. "I don't know anything about your life."

"No. You don't have any idea." Karen's eyes fill with tears. "It's not just the disease. It's everything. It's so loud, all the time." She pushes the button again, but nothing comes.

Dr. Wren has put her cool hands on Karen's face, fingertips to cheekbones. She looks at Karen with a mixture of pity and love. Yes, love.

"My whole life has been bad," says Karen. "Every day is worse. I'm going to a better place. A place where I have dignity, not searches, and needles." She stops, her throat hot. "I deserve that," she says.

"But what if there's nothing?"

Karen looks into Dr. Wren's fearful eyes. "Sometimes I can't wait to die," she says.

"You don't mean that, Karen."

"There is so much more than this world," says Karen.

"I don't know."

"You're so afraid," says Karen. "Listen. Don't be afraid."

Karen watches Dr. Wren, daring her to look away. After a time, she does.

franny

Mid-August in Gatestown: wet thighs, pulsing pavement, heat that grabs you by the throat. Franny woke each morning with her hair plastered across her face. She dreamt of drowning, long dreams where her hair caught on coral or she found herself underneath a wooden dock, unable to find a place where the water ended and she could breathe.

She filled her tub with ice and cold water and spent her evenings reading naked, sucking ice cubes, crushing them with her teeth.

Oh God, it was hot. It was too hot to drink, too hot to eat. Every thought started with a promise and ended with heat: For dinner maybe I—oh fuck, it's hot. Should I have married—Jesus, could it be any hotter? I need to do some laundry, but my skin is melting off my face it is *so damn hot.*

It must have been hot in her childhood, of course it had been. But Franny could not remember it being so ever-present, like smoke in her mind, taking up all the room. Franny was too hot to make lists, too hot to think clearly.

Her happiest moments were in Uncle Jack's Cadillac, driving, when the air-conditioning began to kick in.

One morning, before she opened her eyes, a memory came to her unbidden: the smell of paper and a faint breeze as her mother turned the pages of a new book. Her mother's voice, her breath as she read to Franny, who lay with her cheek on her mother's thigh. Heat, pressing down, and a moment of peace.

Franny sat up in bed. She could see the sun shimmering through her window. She thought of Karen in her dark cell. Franny ran her hand along her sheets, took a sip of the water she kept on the wooden bedside table. Perhaps reading to Karen could help her escape, at least for a few minutes. Franny picked up *One Hundred Years of Solitude*. The library book jacket was laminated and shiny. The pages were cream-colored, stained with age and light.

As Franny walked down the hallway of general inmates, she felt a sense of foreboding. She dealt with these women every day, and smelled the disinfectant, the sex on their skin. She had grown accustomed to the screams, the banging, but she felt scared all the same.

Her footsteps echoed, and Franny was again enveloped in memory, that rich coat: hiding underneath her sheets, reading with a flashlight, the noise of the television coming from downstairs. The sound of someone walking along the hallway to her room. Sheets pulled back with a rough movement, a face in the darkness. A flash of fear, then a calm. Uncle Jack's face, assembled in shadow. He takes the book and the flashlight. But instead of spanking her, or turning off the light, he settles beside her on the bed, and begins to read aloud.

Franny moved briskly past the row of cells. The guards looked at her curiously, but let her pass. At the gate to Death Row, she signed a book—Dr. Wren, 8/17, 2:35pm— and the gate was opened, slid back by a guard, a slight woman with short blonde hair. How had she ended up here, as a guard in Mountain View Unit, waiting in a metal chair, hour after hour, for something terrible to happen? Franny looked at her familiar face—had they known each other as children?—but the woman looked at her impassively, and Franny turned away. She walked through the open gate, and stood on Death Row.

The prisoners looked up. There was the new one, Samantha, doing leg lifts in her cell, flipping through a *TV Guide*. She flashed a dazzling smile and waved like the Queen Mother, fingers cupped.

"Karen, your doctor's here," called a high-pitched voice: Tiffany. She looked so normal, reading a Bible propped up in bed. She twirled a strand of hair around her index finger. What was inside Tiffany that had driven her to take her children's heads in her hands, to hold them underwater until they stopped struggling?

Behind the bars, Karen stood, brought her fingers up to grip the metal. She had been asleep. Her hair was matted and her eyes puffy, but she gazed at Franny with an openness, an earnestness that made Franny embarrassed. Karen's bones had become visible, especially in her face, and her mouth was covered with sores. It was the end of the disease. The morphine canister hummed in the corner of Karen's cell.

"I came to read to you," said Franny.

Karen's brow furrowed. "What?" she said.

"Just be still," said Franny. She sat on a patio chair, and opened the book.

"Ellen's book," said Karen. She looked confused, but nodded, lay back down on her bed and closed her eyes.

Franny cleared her throat, and began to read.

celia

Here I am, in the car, driving. I was watching the news when I heard about Karen Lowens' final appeal. I told myself that I needed an ice cream cone, and that Priscilla needed to come along. She leapt into the jump seat, and I put the truck in reverse and backed out of the driveway. I rolled down the window, and told Mrs. Murphy, who was sitting on her front step, that I was just headed over to Amy's Ice Cream. I sounded cheery, and indeed, I felt cheery. But there is a fine line between cheery and psychotic.

I drove innocently up my street and past Nopalito's and Jovita's, past the Happy Mexican Gas Mart. I turned on the radio and it was the Led Zeppelin that did it. I began to sing, and to ignore the nervous looks Priscilla was giving me. Eventually, she sighed and fell asleep in the back. By this point, we were way past Amy's Ice Cream. We were on our way to Gatestown, Texas, and to Karen Lowens.

I am not quite sure what I have to say to this woman, or why I need to see her. In my mind, both Henry and Maureen beg me to turn around. My mother is packing her little outfits. ("What do they *wear* in Texas in the summer?" she called to ask me. I told her: eyeshadow.) Some lawyer named Rick Underwood is hoping that I'm writing a letter to the governor to beg for mercy. Hah!

Driving gives me time to think. The fact is that in the abstract, I do believe in mercy. I believe people with painful diseases should be able to end their lives. I believe people make mistakes, and that they should be given a chance to atone. But I also feel that something was taken away from me—every fucking thing, in fact—and that I deserve something back. It's a simple equation, a word problem:

Celia Mills has one happy marriage, one mediocre job, one dog, and ten apples. If her husband is shot in a convenience store, what is Celia left with? Express your answer in numeric form.

What is the answer? What do I deserve? When a car blows a tire and a child is killed, the parents sue. The worth of their child's life is defined in dollars. When an employee pinches another employee's ass, that pinch is assigned a specific value in a lawsuit. What it comes down to is this: If Karen Lowens lives, it means that Henry's life was not worth anything at all.

I stop in Georgetown, about a half-hour outside of Austin, for Priscilla to pee. Standing next to a pathetic patch of grass, hoping it will suffice, I feel incredibly tired. The problem in my equation is that if Karen Lowens dies, I don't gain anything. Will it all be over then? Will I be able to move on with my life, and hope for another chance at a happy home filled with babies and juice boxes? Why would her death free me in any way? As Priscilla finally gets down to business, I decide I need a Big Gulp Coke.

I had wanted kids since the day I met Henry. He was a walking advertisement for a future dad. He loved toys, had a grin a mile wide, and liked to pretend he was various animals. (Calling me his "little armadillo," for example, or "mousekin.") Henry wanted to wait, though, until he had decided whether he could stick with programming instead of composing. He wanted to save money and then give himself one six-month blast of free time to see what he could come up with. After that, he promised, we could see about children. He didn't want to be a father who had given up on any dreams. He was the sort who went full-force into anything he set his mind to.

So we waited. It made sense. Add that into the equation: the children we would never have. Henry, holding our baby—that too, was taken away.

karen

After years of minutes and days and words, Karen has a week to live. It is Monday, August eighteenth. In five or six days, over the weekend, she will be taken to Huntsville, and then she will be executed. The HIV in her bloodstream has turned her body against itself, but none of that matters now, not even the unbelievable pain. Dr. Wren comes and ups the morphine.

Dr. Wren also reads to her, sitting outside her cell and crossing her long legs, resting one small shoe on the concrete. Karen does not listen to the words. Instead, she listens to Dr. Wren's voice. She can hear the unhappiness trapped in Dr. Wren's vowels, the fear between her syllables. But Dr. Wren keeps talking, giving Karen stories. Karen is still not sure why Ellen gave her this book, but she is glad for the solace it brings her now.

God gives Karen visions of heaven, telling her it is time. When she wakes some mornings, a bright light fills her eyes instead of the bars, the concrete floor, the guard's sour face.

When prison noises become too loud, God fills her ears with a soft, white noise.

On Monday, Rick Underwood comes to see Karen. The guards put her in a wheelchair—she is too weak to walk now—and bring her to the visiting room. "Oh God," he says, when he sees her. "Oh, Karen, honey."

"Rick," says Karen. She tries to smile.

"Karen, I'm here with bad news," says Rick. "Your appeal was denied."

He says some other things, about faith, hope, heaven, et cetera. Karen closes her eyes and listens as his words swim around her. She knows it all, inside, where it matters. The words are cheap.

It hurts Karen to breathe, and to talk. She has thrush in her mouth; it has a yeasty taste. If she closes her eyes for too long, she can see the faces. They will surround her at the execution: the wives, Ellen, the living, the dead, watching her, waiting for her to be gone. Waiting for the chemicals to course through her brain, and burn her heart still.

That night, Tiffany and Sharleen get into a screaming argument about God. Tiffany has gone whole hog for Jesus. She has gotten serious about Bible study, and on the occasions she does not quote God, she quotes Moira. She wants desperately to save Sharleen, and tells her God will grant Karen a stay of execution. Sharleen says this is bullshit.

"Don't blame me when you end up in hell!" cries Tiffany. "Satan Killer," she adds.

"You talking to me?" says Sharleen.

"Fuck yes, I am." Tiffany's eyes are wet, and her face is flushed. She is standing with her fists balled up.

"You're losing it, Tiff," says Veronica, who sits at the metal table.

"*You know I'm crazy for you!*" belts Samantha. Her habit of singing loudly unnerves everyone. They are waiting for her to drop the act: if she were really crazy, she wouldn't be on Death Row.

Veronica gives Karen a piece of lined paper and a crayon. Karen writes:

Dear Ellen,

I don't know if you have herd, but I am going to be executed on August 25. I remmember our nites together during the summer. Like that time when you wrote the pome and read it to me. You said I was a firefly. Do you remmember? I am allowed guests to come to the execution. Would you come? I would like you there, making sure I will go to heven. Will you come? Please. I will put your name down.

Love,
Karen

So far, only Rick is coming to the execution. And the wives, of course, the wives.

franny

As Franny hurried to the parking lot, her mind was filled with numbers. T-cell counts and the machine code and the number of minutes that Karen would live. She almost ran straight into Rick Underwood, came face to face with his ketchup-stained shirt. Franny looked up. "Hot dog for lunch?" she said, pointing.

He looked down. "Hamburger," he said sheepishly.

Franny laughed. She could feel the heat invading her clothes, filling every fold. "I've been waiting for you," said Rick. "You work late."

"It's seven-fifteen," said Franny.

"Never met a workaholic I didn't like," said Rick. "Do you have time for a beer?"

"Hell, yes," she said.

They picked up Budweiser, chips, and salsa at the Spurs Gas Mart and went to sit in Raby Park, on broken bleachers overlooking an empty pool. Franny opened the salsa and ate a chip. She saw Rick reach out to her, but he stopped himself, dropped his hand.

"You have salsa on your chin," he said.

"Thanks," said Franny.

"Karen looks awful," he said, opening his beer.

"Better keep your can in the paper bag," said Franny. "I wouldn't want you to get in trouble with the law."

"Franny—"

"I know," said Franny. "I'm sorry. When things are hard for me, I make jokes." She sighed. "She's in terrible shape. I'm afraid it's a matter of keeping her out of pain now." She blinked rapidly.

"How long does she have?"

Franny drank the beer. It was cold in her mouth. She held the can to her forehead. "A week?" she said. "Two, maybe. You never know. She could hang on. But she's in pain. I've got her on a constant morphine drip."

"The governor denied her appeal," said Rick, his voice hard.

"I'm so sorry."

Rick turned to Franny. "I know you wrote a letter," he said. "And thank you."

"How did you know?"

He shrugged. "I have sources," he said. He finished his beer. "There's still the possibility of a stay. Who wouldn't just let her go on her own? What's the point of the show?"

"I don't know," said Franny. For a time, they sat in silence, watching the sun fade.

"Well," said Franny. She stood.

"Thanks for your time, Franny."

"It's fine."

"Do you…do you have time for dinner?"

Franny looked down at him: his eyes so bright, his stubbled cheeks, smooth lips.

"No," she said. "I'm really busy these days."

"Of course." He nodded.

"Take care," said Franny, and then she left him. She left him to watch the sun go down.

Franny returned home to find a letter from Nat in the mailbox. She sat down at the kitchen table, mixed a glass of whiskey and Tab, and read:

Fran,

Even though I packed your things, I was waiting for you to come home. Stupid me. I've finally realized that you are not capable of loving anyone. It has taken me this long. I was the last one who believed in you. I didn't believe that you would just head off without any thoughts of the pain you'd cause me, my parents, our friends.

I am sorry for you. I truly pity you. Whatever happened to you when you were young froze your heart, Franny. I thought I could open you up to love but it's impossible. I hope you have a cold, lonely life, you heartless bitch.

Nat

Franny read the letter twice. She traced the movements of his scrawling pen. She took a deep breath, and then she folded the letter, put it back in its envelope, and threw it away in the plastic trash bin. Then she took the bin, carried it outside to the garbage can, and dumped it out. She changed out of her work clothes, and she headed for the Gatestown Motor Inn Lounge.

celia

"**B**ut I went and bought cowboy boots already," says my mother when I tell her I no longer need her to come to Texas.

"There's still another week until the execution," I tell her, "and I'm hanging in there. They've asked me to come back to the library. I was just having a bad night."

This is a complete lie. As I talk to my mother, I am sitting with Priscilla in a moldy motel room in Gatestown, Texas, trying to get the courage to visit the prison and watching soap operas in the meantime. It really is amazing: you can watch soap operas in college, go on with your life for years, get married, get a job, but when the day comes that you turn on the television midday, you can catch right up.

"If you're sure," says my mother. I can see her making lunch dates at the club already, looking forward to spilling the story about her wacko daughter in Texas whom she didn't have to go visit after all.

"I am," I tell her, in as sane a voice as I can muster. "I really am fine."

"I'm so glad," she says.

When I hang up the phone, Priscilla shoots me a warning look. I throw her the rest of my cheeseburger. I call the prison, and finally get the warden, a woman with a calm voice, on the phone. She tells me that Karen has to put me on a visitors' list. She will talk to Karen for me, she says. I leave the motel phone number, and the warden promises to call me back.

There's a bar on the ground floor of my motel, and when I walk in, some skeevy men look me up and down. What if I had some sex in Gatestown, and then went home, I wonder. Even in my condition (horny), none of the candidates looks too appealing. And Priscilla would hate me.

At the bar, a disheveled-looking brunette woman about my age sits nursing a Scotch. I slide onto a stool next to her and a boy who looks way too young to be anywhere near a beer, much less a wall of liquor bottles, comes over to tend to me. "Are you visiting?" he asks, as he pours me a Coke. (Despite the Big Gulp Coke, and three more on the drive to Gatestown, I slept soundly as soon as I nestled next to Priscilla in my motel bed. There is something about motel beds that I adore. The clean sheets, the foam pillows.)

"Yes," I say. "I'm here visiting."

"Hm," says the boy. He brings me some peanuts. The look I give him works, and he walks away.

The disheveled woman looks me over in a covert manner. Is she going to hit on me now? Maybe I'm sending out vibes after all. But she turns away and then signals to the bartender for another Scotch. She does not look good.

I am still not sure what I am doing in Gatestown. The neon bar signs seem too bright, and the jukebox is playing old country shit. All of the seedy-looking men at the tables, most of them in those shiny suits you can get at Sam's Club for $19.99, make me feel that I am at a low point of my life. I will not, with all probability, look back on this evening as one where I felt my personal best, even if I do boot the little pooch from my bed and replace her with one of the slicksters.

"Visiting the prison?" says the disheveled lady. I nod and sip my Coke. This town is seriously weird. "I work at the prison," says the woman.

"Really," I say. But I say it in such a way that it is not a question inviting more commentary. More of an abrupt *I-don't-really-care*. I am not interested in getting chummy with prison officials.

"Yes," she says. "They're executing one of my patients next week."

I look at the woman. Her hair is pulled into a ponytail with a rubber band. She wears jeans, sneakers, and a little pink T-shirt. "You know Karen Lowens?" I say.

She nods. "It's so sad," she says. And she takes a big mouthful of her drink.

A large woman in a muumuu comes into the lounge through a side door, carrying sheet music. She drops her duffel bag by the piano and disappears into the Ladies' Room.

"What's she like?" I say.

"Karen? She's…there's something about her. You can

see who she was as a child. Before she became…what she became. And now, of course, she's very sick."

"Really?" I say, interested this time.

She nods. "AIDS," she says. "The last stages. Terrible pain." The woman is slurring a bit. "I've got her on a morphine drip. She's half gone already." She shakes her head. "And they just denied her last appeal."

This is news to me. I can't tell if I am happy or sad. Neither, I decide.

"She just wants to die," the woman continues. "She's going to die. But why the state has to do it for her I don't know."

"She is a murderer," I say.

The woman looks at me blearily. "I know," she says. "But it just seems so strange to me. I mean, who is it going to help to kill this sick woman? How is that going to make any difference to anyone?"

She has me there. I don't have an answer for that one.

"I mean," says the woman, finishing her Scotch and wiping her lips with the back of her hand, "I mean, is holding a grudge helping anyone?" Maybe something shows in my face. I am not crying. My eyes are dry as a bone. "I'm so sorry," says the woman. "It's been a terrible day. Please forgive me."

"How about another drink?" I say.

I begin to drink, too. The woman and I drink until the piano lady starts playing a medley of show tunes: "Anything Goes," "Luck Be a Lady Tonight," "Memories," "At the Ballet." We sit next to each other at the bar, and we drink.

The woman goes on and on about Karen Lowens. She tells me about the code to the morphine machine that she has written in a little red book, and how much she wants to give the code to Karen and let Karen commit suicide. Karen could program the machine up to a lethal dose, the woman explains drunkenly. "She could let herself go when she wanted to," says the woman. "She's seen me use the machine," she says. "Karen knows how to use it."

The woman still hopes the governor will issue a stay, and that she will be able to cure Karen. The woman begins talking about a child named Anna, about a failed engagement. She gets very, very drunk, and I tie on a nice buzz myself, nodding and listening to the woman, before I lurch upstairs to bed.

karen

Karen's dreams are feverish, melting, surreal. In them, she is on a stage, trying to walk across a tightrope, but the audience in the circus tent keeps screaming and throwing her off-balance. She falls, crying out, and wakes in a sweat, heart thumping.

On Tuesday, Karen has visitors. She brushes out her hair and Tiffany gives her a tube of lipstick, eyeing Karen's sores and telling her the lipstick is hers to keep. Karen is not good in interviews. Rick had told her after the trial that part of the problem was her inability to show emotion. It is the same in interviews. She sits with a face like a stone, licking at her lipstick while the reporters look sympathetic. They all ask her the same things: Are you sorry? *Yes.* Are you scared? *Yes.* Do you think the governor will give you a last-minute stay? *I pray that he will take mercy on me and let me die in peace.*

Even the guards are nice to Karen now, slipping her an

extra apple with lunch (which she cannot eat), not hurting her in the searches. They are afraid of her. Everyone is surprised that the television talks about her so much. She is not pretty, and her story is just plain sad, not lurid like the stories of Jackie and Samantha, who dropped her son out a window.

And Karen gets letters. Crazy people write her letters, telling her that she is a savior or she is going to hell. Even a man who says he is Karen's cousin comes to visit, and sits behind the glass and talks about family. Karen doesn't want to upset anyone, so she just sits and listens. Finally, she stops seeing visitors. She stops getting out of bed. She has begun the wasting sickness, the shits. Sweating, when it is cold as ice inside her. Ellen has not written back.

Dr. Wren comes to Karen every day, to read *One Hundred Years of Solitude*, which is some kind of fucked-up story full of magic and doomed love. Sometimes, Karen pretends that Dr. Wren is an angel, and sometimes she pretends it is Ellen, reading to her, soothing her.

Noise. Phone calls, visitors, radio shows, TV. The media makes Karen what they want her to be:

"This serial killer is manipulating the system, taunting the American public. She says she wants mercy. Well, she should have thought of that before she killed all those men." Republican House Leader Peter Weston.

"Her inner child is hurting. She is fighting back, trying to punish the mother. In this case, the mother is the state of Texas. It's quite complicated." Self-Help Author Liza Weebs.

"The fact is that she is extremely ill. If the governor were to grant her a stay, it might give her some faith. It might give us all some faith." Rick Underwood, Attorney.

"She was always kinda weird. Bought lots of champagne." Sandi MacElroy, Manager, Hi-D-Ho Motel & Mini-Mart.

"I pray for Jesus to save her soul, as well as my own." Tiffany Brooks, in the *Free Tiffany Newsletter,* August Issue (never published).

"She did it all for love. And I think that is so cool. She's like Juliet, and she's going to die for love. Also like my friend Jen, who OD'd on aspirin when Kenny dumped her." Local Gatestown Teen, Jill Marquie.

"She, she dragged my husband into the bushes! She took his wedding ring! My God, she is a menace to society. Speaking for my entire family, we want Karen Lowens to fry so that there can be peace in Texas." Sarah Kellerman, wife of victim number three, Elliott Kellerman.

Karen just wants the noise to stop.

On Thursday afternoon, Warden Gaddon comes to see Karen. She approaches Karen's cell, her eyes are kind. Karen tries to stand up, but cannot find the strength. Warden Gaddon unlocks Karen's cell and steps inside. She stands at the foot of Karen's bed. "How are you feeling?" she asks.

"Bad," says Karen. The warden smells of grass and starch.

"Karen, I know you've decided not to have any more visitors, but there's someone who keeps calling, and I promised her I'd come and talk with you."

"Ellen?" Ellen's face swims in Karen's mind.

"No, Karen, it's Celia Mills. Her husband was Henry Mills." The beautiful woman, the one who had written the letter. "It's completely up to you, Karen," says the warden. "But Celia Mills thinks it might help her if she could speak with you. And maybe it would bring you some peace, as well."

Karen does not answer.

"I'll let you think about it," says the warden. She stands, and steps outside the cell.

"Yes," says Karen. "Tell her I'll see her."

"Are you sure?"

Karen begins to cough. "Yes," she says, between breaths.

"I'll arrange it, then," says the warden.

That afternoon, when Dr. Wren pauses in her reading, Karen says, "Dr. Wren?"

Dr. Wren hooks her finger in the book to mark her place and closes it. "Karen," she says, "call me Franny."

"I don't have anyone…to come to the execution. Could you…"

Franny nods. "I'll be there," she says.

And then it is Friday. They will take her sometime over the weekend to Huntsville. Dr. Wren—Franny—tells her that there are picketers outside the prison, dozens of them. They hold signs asking for mercy for Karen. Karen starts to cry. "Will they give me a stay?" she asks. Her coughs rack her body.

"Oh, Karen," says Dr. Wren, "I hope so."

◆ ◆ ◆

At the end of her visit on Friday, Dr. Wren reaches through the bars and takes Karen's hand in her own. "I can't come to see you anymore," says Dr. Wren. She looks terrible, and smells of old whiskey. "Until Huntsville," she adds.

"I know."

"I wish there was something I could say. I don't know," she says quietly, "how to say goodbye." Karen does not meet her gaze. After a moment, Dr. Wren lets go of Karen's hand. "I will be there with you," she says. "You will not be alone, Karen."

Karen lies awake all night, wishing she had answered Dr. Wren. Wishing she had said, "I love you. I am ready. Let me go."

franny

Franny drove slowly away from the prison. She was over-whelmed with frustration. She had tried to keep herself insulated, and here she was again, heartbroken. Karen would be dead in three days.

When Franny saw the full parking lot at the Motor Inn, she wanted to cry. She could not bear it: the full bar, the men in shiny suits and the women with heavy makeup. She winced at the memory of her drunken rambling to that pretty woman. How humiliating.

She pulled into the gas station, fumbling through scraps of paper in her purse until she found Rick's number. He answered on the first ring.

"Rick? It's Franny Wren."

"Oh, hello, Franny."

"Rick," said Franny. "Isn't there anything we can do? I just…"

"Why don't you come over?" said Rick.

"Over where?"

"To my house. I live in Waco." He cleared his throat. "It's about an hour," he said. "I suppose you couldn't…"

"No," said Franny. "I'd like that. They won't let me see her…until…"

"I know. Until Huntsville. I could—I'll have dinner waiting. We can go to Huntsville together in the morning. You can sleep on my couch."

He gave her directions. As Franny scribbled them onto her hand with a ballpoint pen, she realized that this was crazy, driving to a strange man's house in another town, sleeping on his couch. But he was the only one who would understand. Also, she wanted to drive, and desperately needed a destination.

In the gas station, she bought a Snickers bar. She turned her radio up loud, and rolled down the windows. The hot air came over her face in waves, and she sang until her voice grew hoarse: *I left something turned on at home! Well it isn't the coffee pot, it isn't the heater. She's a whole lot cuter and a whole lot sweeter…I left something turned on at home!*

Franny had spent some time in Waco as a child, but not much: choral recitals, soccer tournaments. Rick lived near the main square. His house was small, yellow with green shutters. In the last light, the lawn was tinted crimson. Franny turned into the driveway, and the gravel made a crunching sound. Rick opened the front door and came out to greet her, a pair of barbecue tongs in his hand. Franny smiled at the sight of him. He wore flip-flops, and cotton shorts with a threadbare T-shirt that said LONGHORNS.

Franny stepped from the car, and Rick said, "Ribs?"

"What?"

"You like ribs?" He looked worried.

Franny laughed. "I love them," she said.

Rick's backyard had a huge cactus garden, which he had strung with white lights. Franny settled into a lawn chair, and Rick handed her a cold mug of beer. The heat was dissipating slowly now that the sun had set, but Franny's skin was damp, her skirt sticking to her legs. A large smoker took center stage in the middle of Rick's patio, and he tended lovingly to the ribs, brushing sauce onto them from a yellow bowl. He had put on music (some of the rocks around the patio appeared to be speakers), and Lyle Lovett sang plaintively.

"So, you're a native New Yorker?" said Rick, looking at Franny over his shoulder.

"Are you kidding? I grew up in Gatestown." Franny smiled at the look on Rick's face. His hair curled in the humid, evening air.

"And I thought I was making ribs for a New Yorker," said Rick, shaking his head, "Now the pressure's on." He paused. "So Dr. Wren was your father's brother?"

"Yes." Franny did not add, *and my father and mother.*

They talked about nothing for a while: football, Rick's law school years at U.T., the weather, the lack of Chinese food in Texas. Franny felt relaxed in a way she had not felt in a long time, and found that she did not want to leave Rick's backyard. Even as she sat underneath his oak trees, stars beginning to sparkle through the leaves, she was dreading the time when she would have to return to Uncle Jack's lonely house, the reporters, and the motel bar.

"So how long are you planning to stay here?" Rick asked.

"I'm not sure," said Franny. "Now that I've got my cat, I don't have a whole lot to go back to. Uncle Jack had a private practice here, on Fifth Street. I've thought about re-opening it, but I don't know."

Rick set the glass-topped table with yellow plates, and brought out steaming corn, potato salad, and a plate of Wonder Bread slices piled high. He set the glistening ribs on a tray. Franny savored her first bite. "These are almost as good as my Uncle Jack's," she said.

"Dr. Wren?"

"He raised me, actually. Rick, both my parents died in a car accident when I was six years old."

"I'm so sorry."

Franny nodded. She took a breath. "Uncle Jack sent me away to school when I was sixteen," she said, "but somehow this feels like my home."

"Really?"

Franny blushed. "I mean Texas," she said.

"Of course."

"There was a settlement, after my parents' deaths. It was spent on my education. His idea was to get me out of here. But somehow I've always felt...I don't know how to explain it."

"Indebted?"

Franny nodded. "Yeah. As if I owed something. I never

asked for the money, but since it came from…" Franny stopped.

"You've done so much," said Rick. "Look at what you've done for Karen."

Franny took a deep breath. "If only I could do more," she said.

"I know," said Rick. "I know what you mean."

Franny wiped her eyes, and then her salty lips with a napkin. They were silent for a few minutes, and then Franny said, "So, how long have you lived in Waco?"

"Since law school. I followed my wife here."

"You were married?"

"Yes. Carolyn. It didn't end well. I was—still am, I guess—too tied up in my work. I didn't have anything left for her." He shook his head. "It was a crazy time. There was a fellow on Death Row—Kit Gantry."

"Oh, my God," said Franny. "You're…"

Rick laughed. "Kit Gantry's lawyer," he said. "Yes, I am. I was."

"And you got him off Death Row!"

Rick smiled. "He lives in Galveston now," he said. "Just sent me a picture of his new granddaughter."

"How amazing," said Franny. "I read all about it."

Rick sighed. "It was eight years ago," he said. "Gantry's sister contacted me, swore he was innocent. I believed her." He leaned back in his chair, told Franny about the DNA findings, the judge who ruled they were admissible, the day Gantry was released from Death Row.

"My wife," said Rick, "was left out, angry. But I really

thought it was the beginning of something, my great crusade." He smiled sadly. "And how can I come home for dinner when someone's life is on the line?"

Franny nodded. "It must have been very hard," she said.

"Well, that was eight years ago," said Rick. He sighed. "What seemed like the beginning turned out to be my last hurrah."

"I remember reading about the Gantry case. It was all over the papers, even in New York. You saved a man's life, Rick."

"And I've watched many die, unable to do a damn thing."

"But you keep trying."

Rick smiled. "Yes," he said. "I do keep trying."

Franny thought about Anna, about Karen and her visions of heaven. The corn was sweet and buttery, and Franny ate.

Rick brought out a pan of bread pudding and hot brandy sauce. "No," said Franny. "I can't eat any more."

"Well, I'll leave it here, just in case," he said, spooning himself a large portion.

The smells mixed together: the smoker, the brandy sauce, the brown sugar in the bread pudding. The beer, and Rick's own scent, a strong smell of cinnamon and smoke. Franny leaned back in her chair and looked at the stars. She laughed.

"What's so funny?"

"Oh, I'm just happy, I guess," said Franny.

"I'm so glad," said Rick. "What a wonderful thing to hear."

There was another silence, and then Franny spoke. "She's going to die, isn't she?"

"Well, there aren't any appeals left. And the governor. Franny, he's not going to issue a stay."

"But someone could—isn't there anyone—"

"No," said Rick. After a few minutes, he said, "She might get a stay. Why don't we just hope for that, Franny?"

Franny did not answer.

Rick made her a bed on the couch, clean blue sheets and a pillow. The living room had pine floors and a large painting hung over the fireplace. It was a painting of a house surrounded by wildflowers. "That's our family ranch in Dripping Springs," said Rick. "One of my nieces painted it."

"It's lovely."

"We've got bluebonnets," said Rick. "Lady Bird made sure of that." He finished making her bed.

"Do you want kids?" said Franny.

"God, yes," said Rick, with a yearning in his voice that surprised her. "I mean," he said, clearing his throat, "you know, who doesn't?" He laughed. "Anyway, you can change in the bathroom. I'll put a T-shirt and some shorts out for you."

"Thanks, Rick."

"Well." He paused, and Franny felt the connection between them, a tender warmth, a glimpse of joy. Rick looked at her, and then he looked away. "Goodnight, Franny," he said.

"Yes," said Franny. "Goodnight."

Rick's bathroom was clean, a bar of Ivory soap by the sink. Franny took a towel and brought it to her face, breathing in Rick's cinnamon smell.

On the couch, Franny found a Longhorns soccer T-shirt and blue boxer shorts. She changed in the dark, wondering if Rick was listening to her movements.

Franny could see stars outside the window, and hear crickets. She fell asleep in minutes.

In the morning, Franny smelled bacon, and, for the first time in a long time, she looked forward to getting out of bed. She found Rick in the kitchen frying eggs. "Coffee's in the pot," he said gruffly, but then he turned to her. "You drink coffee?" he asked, his eyebrows raised.

"Yes," said Franny, pouring some into a white mug.

"I'm not much of a morning person," said Rick.

Franny laughed. "Fine with me," she said. She took the paper outside and opened it on the glass table. As she turned the pages, she felt Rick watching her through the window.

"Look, she's on the front cover, for Christ's sake," said Franny, when Rick came outside with breakfast on a tray: bacon, eggs, toast, grapefruit.

Rick took the paper. That terrible picture of Karen in the bar was splayed, huge and colorful, under the words, HIWAY HONEY TO GOVERNOR: 'HAVE MERCY ON ME!' Karen's mouth was open, her eyes wild and flashing.

"I hate that fucking picture," said Rick.

According to the paper, hundreds of picketers had gathered in Gatestown, surrounding the prison. "My God," said Franny, "you can't even see the front door. I wish I could be there."

"Don't bother," said Rick. "They won't let you in. Not

anymore. They try to be secretive about when she goes to Huntsville. They stop all visitation."

"We'll see her in Huntsville, right?"

"We'll see her," said Rick. He chewed his bacon angrily. "Gets to me every time," he said. Franny wanted to kiss him, this heavy, fierce man, but she took a forkful of eggs instead.

celia

I leave Priscilla at my crappy motel, and drive slowly to the prison. It is the middle of the day, and the sun is a hard thing, pressing on the windows of my car. The air-conditioning tries desperately to make a dent in the heavy heat. I take a left at a Spurs Gas Mart, and the prisons loom before me in a row. They are brown, circled with barbed-wire fences. In the exercise yards, in August, the ground has turned to dust. The only color is the sky, a pale horizon. I take a right at the end of the road to reach Mountain View Unit.

I know it is Mountain View Unit because there are more guards perched in towers, their guns trained on the roads out. There are rows of fences; climbing one is not enough. I am shaking as I pull up to the guard station.

A short man with big sunglasses looks up from the book he is reading. (It is a Tom Clancy novel, *Without Remorse.*) He takes a clipboard from his desk and walks to my car. He raps on the window. "Oh," I say, and roll it down.

"Name of visitor," he says in a metal monotone.

"Karen Lowens."

When he raises his eyebrow, it is almost imperceptible, but I see it. "Your name," he says.

"Celia Mills." This does not elicit any response, though they have been showing my picture on the news for days. That damn honeymoon picture! If I had known that our honeymoon picture would be all over the news, I certainly would have brushed my hair. (I was astonished when I finally realized how reporters had gotten the picture in the first place: one of Henry's colleagues had taken it off Henry's desk and sold it.)

The man holds the clipboard out for me to sign. I take it, but the pen does not work, no matter how hard I press down. I unlatch the glove compartment to reach for another pen, and before I know it, the guard is barking for me to stay still, and he is reaching for his gun. "I just need a pen," I say.

"Oh," he says. I cannot see his eyes behind the mirrored glasses. He hands me a ballpoint from his pocket. When I hand back the clipboard, he says, "Pop the hood."

"Excuse me?"

"Pop the hood," he says slowly, as if I am a child. I pull the cables, and he takes his time looking at my engine, and then in my back seat. (I try to think of what he's seeing: my gym bag, raincoat, those red high-heels that look fabulous but hurt too much to walk in.)

Finally, he closes my hood and comes back around. "Go ahead," he says.

I drive to the Visitors' Parking Area. When I climb from the car, the heat punches me like a fist. I walk to the prison entrance. From a tower, a guard watches me. His face is blank and his hand is on his rifle. When I lift my hand in greeting, he does not respond.

The door is heavy and the knob is hot. I pull it open, expecting air-conditioning, but it is the same temperature inside as out. The warden is waiting for me. She is a tall, black woman in a neat uniform. She takes my hand in both of hers. She looks tired. "I'm glad to meet you," says the warden. I do not tell her that I find this strange. She asks me if I want to come into her office for a cold drink, gesturing with an elegant turn of her wrist. I say no.

"Karen is expecting you," says the warden. "She's in the visiting room."

The warden sees the flicker of fear across my face. "She's handcuffed, and behind glass," says the warden. "You're completely safe." I nod. I am feeling dizzy.

The visiting room is empty except for two guards and a frail woman in a wheelchair. There is a soda machine in the corner. My eyes adjust to the bright light (the hallways of the prison are dim and close) and I see that the frail woman is Karen Lowens. "Just let the guards know when you're done," says the warden.

"Thank you," I say.

I walk toward the wall of glass and sit in a plastic chair opposite Karen. She watches me. Her face is like a skeleton, and her mouth is wet with sores. Her eyes look hollow. I pick up the receiver.

"Karen?" I say. She nods, and does not say anything. We sit like this, in silence, and her eyes fill with tears.

She says something into the phone, and I press it to my ear. She says, "I wish I hadn't killed him."

It is not enough; it is nothing, and yet something hard inside me yields.

"I got your letter," she says. She looks down. Her wrists are cuffed in metal.

"You never wrote back," I say.

"I didn't know what to say." Again, the long silence. Our eyes are locked, and my heart beats rapidly.

"What did it look like?" I say. "What was it like, for Henry?" I find that I am holding my breath.

Karen begins to speak quickly. "I shot him and he fell," she says. Her voice is dark. "He fell and looked at me. I watched him pass over. He knew and I knew. He closed his eyes. I saw…"

"What?" I say. "What did you see?"

Karen clutches her receiver. She swallows with difficulty. I can see the machine next to her, the morphine machine that the drunk woman at the bar went on about. "I can't," says Karen.

"Karen," I say. "Please tell me what you saw."

Her eyes are wide and confused. She is so close to death. "I saw his soul come up from him," she says.

"What did it look like?"

She told me, but I already knew. "Like lightning," she said.

karen

Karen wakes early on Saturday morning. She is disoriented, pulled from dreams of dark hallways, only the faint sound of guards' voices to keep her company. Suddenly, she is afraid. She hates her life, the noise, the searches, the vomit smell, but what awaits her? Karen presses her lips together. Something bigger, she thinks, something silent, like snow. She has never seen snow. Of course, she has seen it in movies, but not for real. She has never tasted a snowflake, or skated on ice. She touches her book, remembers the words: *that distant afternoon when his father took him to discover ice.*

Breakfast: cereal with warm milk. A guard comes to her. He is red-haired, tall with freckles and glasses. He looks away as he hands her a paper cup, and then walks quickly to his station. Karen holds it between her palms. It is hot, and she takes a sip: strong coffee, full of cream and sugar. Karen gulps it down. She almost cries with gratitude, and then thinks: the guards could have brought her good coffee any day, every day. Only on her last day did they bother.

The other women are quiet all morning, ignoring the blaring television. This is hard on them, Karen knows. They have to stay.

After lunch (sloppy joes, Karen is given two, and then a Hershey bar, which she eats and promptly throws up), they come for her. There is a special guard, who nobody knows, from Huntsville. With him is the guard named Hamm; Karen hears his voice in the hall. The gates sliding, metal on metal. She sits up.

"Karen Lowens?"

"Yes."

They open her cell, take her small box of things. "Can I say goodbye?" asks Karen as they chain her wrists and legs.

"No," says Hamm, but the other says, "Come on, Guy."

They take her arms, pull her up.

"She's supposed to have a wheelchair!" says Tiffany. She is getting hysterical. "She's too weak to walk!"

Hamm sticks his hand under Karen's arm, holding her upright. "She's just fine," he says. Karen feels dizzy, and her knees give, but Hamm does not let her fall. The IV snakes from her arm, and the other guard wheels the machine from her cell.

Tiffany is crying, gripping the bars, her straw-colored hair askew from sleeping. She has stopped painting her nails, stopped her sit-ups. She looks like a hundred other inmates, her splashy beauty drained away. "Oh my God," she says. "Oh my God. Oh my God."

"Hey, hey," says Karen. There are spots swimming in her vision.

"God loves you. He loves you, Karen," says Tiffany.

Veronica is sitting on her bed, touching her permanent ink wedding ring with her thumb. "I'm next, aren't I?" she says. Below her eyes are dark circles. It will be worst for Veronica, thinks Karen. She has false hopes. Veronica still dreams of sleeping next to a warm man, yearns for grass and the sound of birds.

"It's OK," says Karen, lamely.

"See you up there," says Veronica. She stands and reaches for Karen's hand, but Hamm jerks her away. The handcuff bites into her skin, and Karen cries out. Hamm's cheap cologne fills Karen's nostrils. He has combed his hair into a stiff wave for the cameras.

"Guy, come on," says the other guard. Hamm jerks her arm again. Karen grits her teeth, and is silent.

The television is on, a soap opera. A man and a woman drink champagne by candlelight. Karen wants to say goodbye to Sharleen, but Sharleen is asleep. Her face is peaceful. "Goodbye," says Karen.

Sharleen's eyes snap open. "Hey," she says. "Goodbye." Even Sharleen's voice is weak.

Samantha sings as they carry Karen out: *So long, farewell, it's time to say good-night!*

They take Karen into the hallway, past the guards seated at the desk, past the other inmates who scream and bang their bars. The din is unbelievable, they call her name again and again. This time it is *"Karen! Karen!"* and not her nickname. For this, Karen is thankful.

While they fill out paperwork in the narrow hallway,

Karen sits between two guards. One smells of coffee, the other of cologne. Their arms are hot against hers. Karen tries to think about the quiet earth, but there is noise everywhere: women's hoarse voices, televisions, the guards' whispers and occasional barking cries: "Hey! Watch it! I'm warning you, bitch." Karen pushes the black button, and the morphine courses into her bloodstream.

Karen knows that she will have a few seconds, after being led from the prison, but before being put in the van. A few precious seconds to turn her face to the sun, feel the air on her skin, and smell life outside the walls. As they pull her to her feet, and walk down the corridor, she waits.

The doors bang open and it hits her at once: the bright sun, the screaming, signs held high, open mouths, fists rising heavenward. She closes her eyes, raises her face, feels the warmth, and then it is over. Hamm's hard fingers push her head down and she is inside the van, the thick tinted windows sealing her off completely.

She can see the town dimly once her eyes adjust to the van's darkness. Through the back window she sees storefronts, Andy's Home Cookin', the Gatestown Motor Inn. She sees people going about their lives, carrying groceries, mowing the lawn. A boy with a dog on the end of a piece of twine, a woman with a baby in her arms, sitting on her porch, drinking lemonade. They have no idea that they are blessed.

The drive to Huntsville takes five hours. The back of the van is quiet, and Karen closes her eyes, gives herself morphine from the machine, and feels the road beneath them, the bumps, the hissing of the air conditioner. The van smells new, like leather. The handcuffs make her wrists ache. Her mind is blank; she basks in the silence.

The Huntsville Prison is huge and feels sinister, violent. As soon as they take Karen through the front gate, she feels it: death. Two hundred and six men—and one woman, Jackie—have been executed at Huntsville since 1976, some by electrocution, some by firing squad, some by lethal injection.

Karen can smell the scorched hair. She can hear the gunshots ripping through flesh. She remembers reading about Stephen McCoy, who was not given enough drugs in his injection. He choked, began to spasm. A witness fainted. Karen can hear him in the hallways, his pain echoing in her ears. She begins to cough. Her lungs! They have no air. The burned taste of death fills her mouth.

"Shut up, damnit," says Hamm.

"I can't breathe," says Karen. She begins to gasp.

"It's an act," says Hamm. To the alarm of the guards around him, he lets go of Karen's arm. She wobbles on her feet, coughing.

"See?" says Hamm, and then Karen falls. She cannot breathe, she feels her legs collapse, her head hits the floor, and then everything goes black.

franny

When Franny came out of the bathroom, Rick was standing with a hand on the refrigerator, leaning against it. "Rick?" Franny stopped, her hair dripping, a towel wrapped around her.

"Franny," he said. "She's collapsed."

"What?"

"Karen. She's unconscious. She couldn't breathe—hit her head…"

"Where is she?" Franny turned and ran back into the bathroom to gather her clothes.

"The Medical Center at The Walls. As soon as they stabilize her, though, she'll go back to a cell."

"I'm going." Franny pulled on her clothes. When she was dressed, she saw that Rick was holding his car keys.

"Are you coming, Rick?" He shook his head.

"I'm going to the governor. And I'm getting a goddamn stay. They can't pull her out of a coma to kill her."

"They wouldn't."

"Goddamn right," said Rick. "Not if I have anything to do with it."

Franny drove to the prison with the radio off. She rolled down the window, and then rolled it back up. There were so many stoplights. When she hit her third, Franny screamed, "*Come on, for God's sake! Come on!*" and then she began to cry. She chanted, "Come on come on come on…"

Finally, she reached the Huntsville prison, and parked illegally. There was a throng of reporters and picketers outside the front door. "Let me *through*!" she screamed, and some people got out of her way.

"Franny! Franny!" she heard a familiar voice. When she turned, it was Christopher from *News 2*, his microphone in front of her mouth. "Do you have any comments on your patient, Karen Lowens?" he said, motioning for the camera to tape her. Franny looked at him, shocked, and then turned away. But the other reporters had seen, and trailed her. She ran to the prison gate.

"No visitors," said a guard with a terrible complexion and startlingly kind eyes.

"I am her doctor," said Franny. "Let me inside. Now."

The guard looked up with surprise, and respect. "Your name?" he said.

"Dr. Wren," said Franny, feeling proud to have the same name as Uncle Jack.

◆   ◆   ◆

Franny thought she was used to prisons, but The Walls was different. She shuddered as she walked down the rows of bellowing men, finally reaching the Medical Center.

The nurse at the desk wore her hair in a purple band. "I'm here to see Karen Lowens," said Franny, leaning on the counter to catch her breath.

"No visitors," said the nurse, not even looking up from her computer.

"I'm not a visitor," said Franny. After she opened her wallet, explained herself, the nurse let Franny pass.

Karen was still unconscious, threaded with tubes and IV lines. Her face had a bluish tint, the skin pulled tight, eyes sunk deep in her skull. The chart said that she had experienced respiratory failure, collapsed, and hit her head on the floor. Her pneumonia was worse, her lungs filled with fluid.

"Oh, Karen," said Franny. "Hold on. Don't leave me."

"She's due to be executed tomorrow morning," said a man in the corner of the room. Franny recognized him as Guy Hamm, the guard who had shown her around the prison. He was carrying a gun, and his blond hair was wavy and stiff.

"I know," said Franny. She sat by Karen's bedside, holding her hand. Everything she had thought about, worried over, tried to control, had come to this. Holding Karen's hand. Franny was not even sure if she wanted Karen to open her eyes.

From time to time, Karen would writhe and moan, and Franny would program the machine to give Karen a bit more morphine. Franny knew the code by heart. Karen would sigh, and settle back down into her dreams. It would be so easy, thought Franny, to give Karen a high enough dose, to program the machine to give Karen enough morphine to die.

She heard monitors—doctors being paged—and smelled the uneaten meal a nurse had brought for Karen. There was still a chance the governor would issue a stay, and Franny waited. Hamm looked as if he were dozing off.

"Excuse me?" said Franny.

He jerked awake, reaching for his gun.

"I'll be right back," said Franny.

He nodded, blinking. Franny squeezed Karen's hand.

There was no answer on Rick's mobile phone. Franny bought a Twix bar and a cup of coffee and walked down the hallway back to Karen's room. She turned the corner and saw the door to the Medical Center open. Two guards wheeled a gurney, an oxygen tank, and the morphine machine from the room. Franny saw dark hair against the white sheets on the gurney. "Wait!' she cried. The men pushed the stretcher away from Franny, through the swinging doors at the opposite end of the hallway. Franny ran to them.

"What happened?" she asked a nurse, who was changing the sheets on the bed where Karen had been. The nurse flipped a clean sheet in the air, snapped it flat.

"She woke up," said the nurse, tucking in the corners.

In the corner of the dark cell, Karen looked small. She lay on a cot, and the only sound was the morphine dripping through the IV into her arm. They had taken away the oxygen. When she heard the bars slide back, Karen opened her eyes. The orange fire was gone; they were dull and flat. "You can have ten minutes," said the guard, a black man Franny did not recognize.

"Okay," said Franny. She thought, *Not if Rick can get to the governor.* She sat at Karen's side. "Karen, how are you?"

"Ready," said Karen. "God knows I am ready right now." Karen's voice was weak, barely above a whisper. Franny nodded. "I was waiting for you," said Karen.

All the strength was gone from her, Franny could see. The sores were like fire on her face, but it was more than that, more than the bones protruding through her skin. "That priest told me I would go to heaven," said Karen. She coughed. "Heaven is sounding good about now."

"No, Karen. Hold on," said Franny. She was filled with the desire to do something, something to save Karen. To bring her strength in this horrible room that smelled of piss and dark corners.

Karen turned her head toward the ceiling. After a moment, she began to speak. "The worst part," she said, and she was whispering, "is that everybody is going to watch me go." She began to spit the words, as if they tasted bitter. "They're going to put a diaper on me. I've been through everything," she said. "I came out of everything and I found some dignity. Inside. When they stripped me and they put it in me—" She coughed, a long, wet cough. "They couldn't touch it," she said.

She looked at Franny. Franny nodded. "Now it's going

to come out of me," said Karen. "And they'll be watching, all them who tried to take it." Franny thought desperately to find words. "Can you understand?"

"But Karen," she began, in a voice that was pleading and wrong in her ears.

"Don't talk," said Karen. "Just tell me I can go."

Franny closed her mouth.

The phone on the guard's desk rang loudly, and Franny jumped. Karen closed her eyes. "Doctor?" said the guard. "It's for you."

"Hold on," Franny said to Karen. "Just hold on, for me." She touched Karen's face, and it was cold.

Franny stood, walked to the cell door. The guard slid back the bars. Franny exited, and the guard closed the door behind her. Karen began to cough. The receiver was heavy in Franny's hand. "This is Dr. Wren," she said.

"Franny?"

"Rick. What's happening?"

"I'm sorry, Franny. I'm so sorry."

"No."

"I'm sorry," said Rick.

"Goddamn it, she only has a few days—maybe even a few hours! They can't give her that?"

"No. Franny, I went and talked to him myself. It's over."

She began to cry. "Stop it," said Rick. "Franny, stop it."

Franny swallowed. She handed the phone to the guard.

"Doctor," said the guard. "Visiting hours are done. It's time for you to go."

"Let me say goodbye," said Franny.

"Hurry it up, then." He let her into the cell.

"Dr. Wren?" said Karen. "Please let me go now. I'm ready to go."

"Yes," said Franny. "I understand." And standing there, watching the sick woman with the child's eyes, Franny did understand. Karen was filled with grace. It shone through her broken body, and over her mistakes. Franny understood then that grace was not like a present. It could not be given, and it could not be taken away.

"Goodbye," she said.

"Thank you," said Karen. "Goodbye."

"God bless you," said Franny, and she nodded to the guard. He came and unlocked the gate. As she walked down the hallway, she could still hear Karen, breathing.

celia

The woman who shot my husband is being executed today, and all I can think about is what to wear. I am aware this is a shallow concern, and yet there it is. A suit seems too respectful, and sweatpants don't seem to allow for the gravity of the situation. Back in my house in Austin, I try on summer dresses, pantsuits, a pair of decent shorts. (The shorts are quickly thrown on the floor: I cannot wear sneakers or sandals to an execution.)

Shoes. I decide to start at the bottom. Slurping coffee that my mother has made, I survey the bottom of my closet. It is over a hundred degrees, which rules out anything leather. (Open-toed shoes, as well, are out. I don't even want to think about what's on the floor of the prison.) I get on my knees and shove things around. I am nude, fresh from the shower, where I both shampooed and conditioned my hair. I feel as if I'm going on a date. Or to a wedding. I begin to laugh. There is something very wrong with me.

At the back of the closet, I see them. The cotton

espadrilles I had pulled on when I went to the hospital. I had been sitting on the porch swing, throwing a ball to Priscilla. The ball was covered with slobber and mud. I was barefoot, thinking of the beer Henry would bring me. I wasn't thinking of Henry. Wasn't thinking—not then—of his soft lips, his warm neck, the way he abandoned himself to sleep, spreading his limbs across the bed. I was thinking of beer.

The phone rang that night, and I went inside to answer it. I figured it was my mother or my friend Gina who always called with a crisis. (And who, it must be noted, dropped me like a hot potato when I had a crisis of my own.) But it wasn't Gina. It was someone trying to win me back to AT&T phone service. He actually said that, and God knows how I remember, "We want to win you back." Priscilla looked at me mournfully, the ball dropped at my feet. The front door was open, and while the man on the phone kept talking (emboldened by my silence, as they always are, looking for any moment to fill) I looked up and there was a police officer in my doorway.

Henry, I thought immediately. That jackass ran a red light, I thought. How much money did I have for bail, I thought. "Miss Mills, I mean Mrs. Mills?" said the police officer, a young boy really, and something in his face made me drop the phone to the floor. Priscilla curled around my feet: she felt it, too.

"There's been an accident," said the boy.

An accident? It was no accident. It was a bloodbath. I had worn these espadrilles. In them, I had seen my husband dead, stretched out under a white sheet, his face the color of clay but his feet the same. His hands, the same.

I put on the espadrilles, and then the loose dress I had been wearing with them. The last dress Henry had seen me in.

My mother, who surprised me by flying in from Wisconsin for the execution, comes into my room and puts her hand on her hip. "It's time to go," she says. She looks old in the early morning light. We have a long drive ahead, from Austin to Huntsville, and my mother has packed a cooler with drinks and cookies, as if we were going on a picnic. The execution is at eleven.

"It still amazes me that you live here," says my mother, as we wind through the quiet streets of my neighborhood on the way to the freeway. "My daughter," she says. "A Texan." She laughs and then sighs.

I suppose I am a Texan, now. I could have left when Henry died, but I have not. As we drive underneath the large oak trees, their roots a hundred years deep, I can begin to see shards of the life I have ahead of me: my quiet desk at the library, the slight chill of fall. My garden, my porch swing.

My mother and I are silent for most of the drive. She puts her hand on the back of my neck, and does not ask me how I feel.

Henry's parents meet us at the House of Pancakes in Huntsville. By the time we arrive, it is too late to eat. Ursula is lit from within with fury. She wears a black dress and simple pumps. The ponytail that hangs down her back is almost entirely white now. The loss of her son is evident in every line on her face. My heart opens like a flower, and when she rises from the Formica table, I take her in my arms. Neither of us cry.

Henry's father has ordered a plate of pancakes, but has not taken a bite, not even poured the syrup. "Is it time?" he asks. His eyes are ringed with dark circles.

"It's time," I say.

At the prison, we are led into a dark, windowless room and to the front row of folding chairs. I have my mother on one side of me, and Ursula on the other. We lock our fingers together. I can see reporters in some of the back rows, and the drunk brunette doctor from the bar, talking to a large man. Around us, in the front row, I see the other victims' families. Most of them look angry, and many seem filled with Ursula's same fire. It seems a very long time that we stare at an empty gurney, waiting.

"Do you think this will make it better?" I ask Ursula, and she clamps her lips together and shakes her head. It will never be better, she is saying with her eyes, and I know that she is right.

My own mother is stroking my palm with her thumb. From time to time she looks over at me and makes a sound in the back of her throat. She is trying to imagine life without me.

The reporters begin to grow restless as eleven o'clock comes and goes. Their voices murmur in the corners of the room. There is a collective sense that something is very wrong, but we know that all of Karen's appeals have been denied. The clock on the wall ticks, and someone clears their throat. A woman begins to sob quietly.

"What the hell is going on?" says Henry's father. His voice is tight, a coiled spring.

And finally, movement. The warden comes to the center of the room, in front of the gurney. She looks nervous, but holds her shoulders back. "Excuse me?" she says, and silence falls.

"There has been an unforeseen turn of events," she says. Her voice rings out in the quiet room. I can hear my own blood pumping, can feel the pulses of my mother and Ursula in my fingertips. It feels as if we have the same heartbeat. In between the beats, I hear the warden tell us that we cannot watch the execution of Karen Lowens, because Karen Lowens is already dead.

franny

After the announcement, Janice Gaddon let Franny into Karen's cell. Karen's body was there, of course, a large mound underneath the thin sheet. Franny closed her eyes. The cracked concrete tile; a dark, sweet smell.

Franny could never know what Karen felt in her final moments, before she killed herself with the morphine. How did she find out the code to the machine? Franny hadn't let her see it, she was sure.

Rick had gone to see Karen in the late hours of the night. She had been alive, but woozy. He sat by her, prayed for her. Then he had gone to Franny, and in the waiting room, on a metal bench, they had held each other. They had not said a word, had cried and slept and cried again. Rick's body was comforting and warm.

In Karen's cell, Franny realized that her hands were balled into fists. There was no sound in the room. Karen looked asleep. Her eyelids were thin as paper. *I came into* *this world alone, and I've been alone since…*and she had died alone. Franny swallowed tears. She took the sheet, cold as stone in her hand, and pulled it over Karen's face.

There would be questions, so many questions. They would look into every part of Franny's care. They would think that she gave Karen the means with which to end her life. Strangely, none of this bothered Franny. In the end, she would be proven innocent—she had not done anything, after all—and her life would go on. She simply couldn't control who would believe her, and who would not.

Janice placed a hand on Franny's arm. "Karen left this. She said it was for you," she said. It was a tiger made of origami paper, orange and gold, its folds softened from touch. Franny closed her fingers around it. She walked with sure steps past the crowd outside Karen's cell. Rick stood in the hallway, his face pale. Franny had let Karen go, had said goodbye, and was ready. Rick looked up, and Franny walked toward him.

celia

When I am home in Austin, and all my guests have gone, I take Priscilla and some supplies and I visit Henry. He is buried in a sunny graveyard, watched over by oak trees. It took a long time for me to come to him, and I suppose I was waiting for the sadness to end. But sadness isn't something that ends, it just becomes less hard. It melts into an ache that is a part of you.

I have planted tomatoes on Henry's grave. They look strange, amidst the roses and carnations, but they are what Henry would have wanted. They have become large and red. Today, I will pick two of them, and make a salad to bring to the christening of Sean and Jenny's new baby, Alice. I am Alice's godmother, and will hold her while the priest touches her forehead with cold water. I went to Sean and Jenny's house a few weeks ago, and they opened the door, and I walked in.

Priscilla lies next to me on the grass, and we think of things to tell Henry. I tell him about my new job at the hospital library. I let him know where we have been swimming and hiking that week and what I've tried to cook for dinner.

I talk and talk to Henry, but he never comes to me again, not since that last night at the Gatestown Motor Inn Lounge. It's as if I did what he asked of me, and he was able to leave. His lightning became a pale glow that I can still see if I concentrate on the night sky.

I think it bothered him that so many people were going to watch Karen die. The moment we die is a private time, and Henry is the kind of person who would understand that. He came to me, in that crappy little bar in Gatestown, Texas. When the doctor went to the ladies' room, leaving her purse on the table, Henry slid into her seat. His hair was a mess, and he looked as if he needed to shave. He told me to find the red notebook in her bag, to write down the code to the morphine machine. I did as he asked, wrote it in lipstick on a bar napkin and memorized it later. I didn't know, of course, that the last time I would ever see Henry was on an orange barstool.

And I didn't quite know how it was all going to fall into place until I went to visit Karen. It's not that Karen said she was sorry, and I don't think I would have believed her if she had. But something changed in me, and I realized that forgiving Karen was something I had to do for myself. It had nothing to do with her, in the end.

She had clutched the receiver in the visiting room, and told me about watching Henry die. Her face was thin and wasted. I felt Henry's hands on my hair, his fingers touching my scalp, readying me the way he had done when he first took me hiking on a steep trail. "You can do it," he had told me, and he had been right.

He stroked my hair, and Karen looked at me, and I had something to give her. It wasn't anything that I had use for, but to her, it was everything. "Karen," I said.

"Yes?" Her voice, small in the receiver. Her hand, pressing on the glass.

You can do it. I heard him, my beloved one.

I pressed my own hand to the glass. The numbers to the machine lined up in my head. I opened my mouth.

acknowledgments

First and foremost, I would like to thank the women on both sides of prison walls who shared their stories with me. *Sleep Toward Heaven* was written to honor and illuminate their lives. Unending gratitude goes to my mentors, Joan Beattie, Bill Hagen, Jim Shepard, Chris Offutt, Kevin Canty, and Dierdre McNamer. Thank you, Debra Magpie Earling, for reaching to your bookshelf and finding William Stafford. William Kittredge, you showed me by example how to live as a writer. For my fellow writers Ann McGlinn, Joni Wallace, Clay Smith, Jill Marquis, Andrew Sean Greer, Aaron Q. Long, Ed Skoog, Stephen Morison, Woody Kipp, Dennis Hockman, Erica Olsen, Stephen Meyer, Maria Hong, Annie Hartnett, Rhian Ellis, J. Robert Lennon, Sheila Black, Emily Hovland, Dao Strom, Brett Hershey, Laurie Duncan, Andrew Spear, and Martin Wilson, as well as my friends Beth Howells, Jessica Goepfert, Cyndi Bohlin, Sage MacLeod, Dave Ruder, Ariel Anderson, Sarah Knight, Molly

Rauch, Juli Berwald, Jaye Joseph, and Mary Maltbie, I am forever grateful. For supporting me during the winter spent writing this novel, I would like to thank the warm community of Ouray, Colorado, especially the Fairchilds, Muellers, Harts, Tisdales, and Williamses. Thank you, Barbara J. Zitwer. For publishing my short stories, I would like to thank Lee Klein of *Eyeshot*, Whitney Pastorek and Jeff Boison of *Pindeldyboz*, and M. M. M. Hayes of *StoryQuarterly*. I am lucky to work with Michelle Tessler, with whom I hope to share many sangrias, and the offices of Carlisle and Company. I am proud to be published by David Poindexter and the MacAdam/Cage team, who care so much about creating beautiful books. I am blessed to have as my friend and editor Anika Streitfeld, who possesses the rare skill of being both an exacting critic and a firecracker of enthusiasm. Thank you to my family; the Toans (and their stolen television); Bret, Laura, Trey, Rachael, Kit, Barbara, and Larry Meckel (and the Oak Street Writers' Fellowship); Andrea, Gary, and the lovely Lorraine Ward; Isabelle Omeler; the Shaber family; Janice Doherty; Mary and Mark Liu; Peter and Brendan Westley. To my sisters and best friends, Sarah McKay and Liza Ward, thank you for always believing. My heart is for my husband, Tip, who makes every day a celebration. And my greatest thanks goes to my mother and my inspiration, the radiant Mary-Anne Westley.